Edwin R. Heath

Exploration of the River Beni in 1880-1

Edwin R. Heath

Exploration of the River Beni in 1880-1

ISBN/EAN: 9783337238995

Printed in Europe, USA, Canada, Australia, Japan

Cover: Foto ©Andreas Hilbeck / pixelio.de

More available books at **www.hansebooks.com**

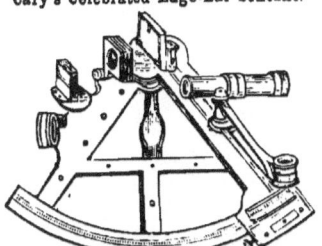

Candidates for admission into the Society must be proposed and seconded by Fellows, and it is necessary that the description and residence of such Candidates should be clearly stated on their Certificates.

It is provided by Chapter IV., § 1, of the Regulations, that,

"Every Ordinary Fellow shall, on his election, be required to pay £3 as his admission fee, and £2 "as his annual contribution for the year ending on the 31st December then next ensuing, or he may "compound either at his entrance by one payment of £28, or at any subsequent period by the payment "of £25, if his entrance fee be already paid."

All Subscriptions are payable in advance, on the 1st of January in each year.

The privileges of a Fellow include admission (with one friend) to all Meetings of the Society, and the use of the Library and Map-room.   Each Fellow is also entitled to receive a copy of the New Monthly Series of the Proceedings and the Supplementary Papers, the former of which is forwarded, free of expense, to addresses in the United Kingdom, and the latter obtained on application at the Society's office.

Copies of the Regulations and Candidates' Certificates may be had on application at the Society's Office, 1, Savile Row, London, W.

PROCEEDINGS

OF THE

ROYAL GEOGRAPHICAL SOCIETY

AND MONTHLY RECORD OF GEOGRAPHY.

The Basins of the Amaru-mayu and the Beni.

By CLEMENTS R. MARKHAM, C.B., Secretary R.G.S.

(Read at the Evening Meeting, April 9th, 1883.)

Map (*Inset Map*), p. 376.

THE receipt of Dr. Heath's diary and valuable maps has brought to our knowledge the achievement of an important feat in South American geography, namely, the discovery of the whole course of the great river Beni. The work of this intrepid explorer will now be brought fully to the notice of the meeting, but its relative significance can only be properly appreciated by considering the physical aspects and the history of discovery over the whole Beni system. From every point of view it is a subject of great interest to the geographer; and moreover it includes the story of other noble exploring adventures hitherto unrecorded by this Society, which deserve a place side by side with the admirable work of Dr. Heath.

The fountains of the Beni system of rivers which supply a large third of the volume of the Madeira, one of the chief tributaries of the Amazons, flow from the great snowy chain of the Eastern Andes for a length of upwards of 500 miles. They converge into two main streams called the Amaru-mayu or Mayu-tata, and the Beni, which, uniting with each other, and then with the Mamoré, combine, with the Itenez, to form the great Madeira river.

The snowy range of the Eastern Andes is an unbroken mass, with a high plateau to the westward and the vast plains of the Amazonian basin to the east. It sends up peaks, such as Illimani and Illampu, to a height exceeding 21,000 feet, and it is remarkable that these towering masses are not bosses of granite, but are of Silurian formation and fossiliferous to their summits. The whole range is highly auriferous, containing frequent veins of gold bearing quartz usually associated with iron pyrites; and the thickness of the strata is not less than 10,000 feet. The main chain is nowhere disturbed by volcanic eruptions, except at the very edge of the formation near Lake Titicaca; and in these respects it differs essentially from the maritime cordillera of the Andes. The characteristics of the Eastern Andes have an influence over the plains which are traversed by rivers flowing from them. The limit of perpetual snow is at 15,800 feet, below which there are steep grassy slopes and precipitous declivities, and thence numerous spurs extend for varying distances into the plain, inclosing profound ravines. It is here that the majestic beauty of the scenery of the Andes is fully realised. Masses of dark mountains rise for thousands of feet, with their bases washed by foaming torrents and their summits terminating in sharp peaks or serrated ridges. The lower slopes are covered with dense vegetation, the green tints often varied by masses of gorgeous flowers; and, above the forest, the grassy slopes are brightened by the yellow of calceolarias and the rich purple of a melastoma. As the ravines are descended the forest becomes more dense, the open glades disappear, and the delicate pink and white of the chinchona blossoms, set in glossy verdure, begin to dot the hill-sides. Everywhere there is flowing water, the condensed moisture of the trade winds hurrying back to the Atlantic. Here is seen a white sheet of continuous foam rushing down the polished side of a precipice and seeming to plunge into a bed of ferns and flowers, there a blue sheet of water appearing to issue from the fleecy clouds that shroud the mountain peaks; everywhere the roar of falling water. As the ravines subside, more extended views are obtained, and at length the vast illimitable plain is seen stretching away in one unbroken forest, the green tints changing to faint blue on the far off horizon. This has ever been a land of mystery, a land to interest and excite the imagination of generations of explorers.

As would naturally be expected, the streams flowing from the auriferous Andes are full of gold. In the ravine of Tipuani the blue clay slates, associated with gold, extend to the river Beni. The gold of Caravaya has been famous for centuries, and in Marcapata is the golden hill of Camanti. But the products of the ravines and of the vast plain beyond are not confined to the precious metal. Gold is far from being the most valuable branch of their varied sources of wealth. This is the region of the chinchona bark richest in quinine, of the finest coffee and cacao in the world, of many kinds of rare and valuable cabinet woods, and of inexhaustible supplies of indiarubber.

The two great rivers to which all the thousand streams, pouring down the eastern slopes of the Andes, converge, are the Beni and the Amaru-mayu, which unite after courses of 500 miles each. One may be said to come from the vicinity of La Paz, the other from the confines of Cuzco, one the outlet for the commercial capital of Bolivia, the other for the ancient capital of Peru. The Beni receives all the streams from near Cochabamba to the frontier of Peru, including those of the famous Yungas of La Paz, and of Ayopaya, Caupolican, Larecaja, Apolobamba, and Munecas. On the Peruvian frontier is the ravine of Tambopata, so rich in chinchona bark, whose river becomes the Madidi, the largest of the Beni tributaries.

The Amaru-mayu has, however, been ascertained by Dr. Heath to be the principal river as regards volume; and this is explained by the physical conformation of the region. The rivers which form the Beni flow direct from the Andes, down ravines, to their parent stream. But in the case of the Amaru-mayu system there is, throughout the provinces of Caravaya and Paucartambo, and beyond the spurs of the Andes, an isolated line of hills running parallel with the main chain. These hills are described as precipitous and gold-bearing, so that they are probably of the same formation as the Andes; but the hills have only once been visited by a scientific traveller, Dr. Don Antonio Raimondi (our Honorary Corresponding Member), in 1864, and his narrative is not yet published. The whole of the rivers of Caravaya are diverted by this isolated range, and form one great stream called the Ynambari, receiving tributaries from both sides, and flowing for a great distance parallel to the Andes, until it forms a junction with the Amaru-mayu coming from the valleys of the Cuzco *montaña*. In consequence of this lateral diversion of the Caravayan rivers, along a distance of nearly 200 miles, a very great volume of water is conveyed to the Amaru-mayu, which swells its dimensions into a noble stream, and gives it a right to claim the Beni as a tributary.

Thus we have to contemplate a portion of the snowy range of the Eastern Andes, the courses of the two great rivers which drain it, with their numerous important tributaries, and the vast unexplored plain stretching away from the bases of the mountains.

There has been a halo of romance resting over this great eastward-stretching plain, like the blue haze on the distant horizon, where the apparently illimitable forests seem to mingle with the sky. The great civilised empire of the Yncas was established on the lofty plateaux to which the Eastern Andes form a bulwark rising out of the forests, and the Yncas were attracted to those rich and unknown regions by the desire to improve the condition of their people as well as by enlightened curiosity. The Yncas formed colonies in all the ravines to the eastward, in accordance with their policy of exchanging products. Each colony came from a particular district on the lofty plateau, and kept up regular communication with the mother village, receiving quinua, preserved potatoes, dried meat, and clothing, and sending in return cabinet woods, medicinal drugs, fruits, coca, and gold.

It was a more formidable undertaking to penetrate far into the forests to the eastward. Here there were perils without end, dangers from wild animals, from savage people, from swollen rivers, and from starvation. But the almost perfect system of land transport and commissariat which formed part of the Ynca system of government, enabled that highly civilised people to overcome them all. In the fifteenth century the Ynca Yupanqui determined to send an expedition to explore the whole region of the Amaru-mayu, or "serpent-river," and learn the secrets of the unknown land beyond the horizon. During two years he caused timber to be cut and dressed, and canoes to be made, while dried provisions were collected. The stores were carried in the centre of each canoe on high platforms, so that they might not get wet. After the expedition started the first work was to overcome the fierce tribes of Chuncho savages who inhabit the forests within 20 miles of the base of the Andes. They were so completely subdued, not so much by force of arms as by wise conciliatory measures, that they gave in their allegiance, adopted agricultural habits, lived in large barrack-like houses 100 feet long, 40 wide, walls six feet high, and good pointed thatched roofs, in accordance with the Ynca system (and continue to do so to this day), and regularly paid tribute in kind until, by the execution of Tupac Amaru, the Ynca rule was unwisely destroyed by the Spanish Viceroy Toledo in 1571.

The Ynca expedition then continued the descent of the great Amaru-mayu river, and completed the discovery. There were serious losses by the way, but about a thousand men reached the country of the Moxos and formed a colony, sending news of their success to Cuzco. The main facts of this expedition are certainly historical. The civilising influence of the Yncas thus spread over the vast plain, and Colonel Church mentions the existence of an ancient Ynca road on the banks of the river Beni.

After the Spanish conquests it was believed that many thousands of the Yncas fled into the forests. Expeditions went in search of them, and there was a tradition of the existence of a fabled Empire of Paytiti beyond the eastern horizon. There was a certain basis of truth in those stories. But the stern facts during Spanish times were that the savage Chuncho Indians encroached more and more on the few coca and cacao farms near the base of the Andes, that the missionaries alone succeeded in penetrating to any distance, and that the bark-collectors and gold-seekers scarcely ever went beyond the outer spurs of the mountains. It was not the policy of the colonial government of Spain to seek new routes for commerce.

As soon as the independence of Peru and Bolivia was established, the people began to desire very earnestly that a highway should be opened for them to the Atlantic. They saw that their prosperity and advancement mainly depended on that great measure, and that there could be no real progress for them until it was secured. Their own efforts have not been wanting. Especially have the people of Cuzco worked zealously to explore their forests, and examine the course of the Amaru-mayu river.

In 1835 our gallant countryman, General Miller, conceived the idea of planting a military colony on the banks of some navigable river on the eastern slopes of the Andes, to facilitate the discovery of the vast plains towards the Madeira, and to endeavour to open a direct communication with Europe by the Amazons. He was Prefect of Cuzco at the time, and he made a journey into the forests of Paucartambo, an account of which was published in our 'Transactions'* but he was unable to give permanent effect to his well-conceived plans. He treated the Chunchos kindly, and they continued to be friendly during his sojourn in their neighbourhood, although they were opposed to his further advance.

But after 1840, they began to make persistent attacks on the few estates near the base of the Andes, destroying several, and spreading consternation over the whole district. The Peruvian Government then commissioned Colonel Espinar, of Cuzco, to visit the remaining farms and report on the state of affairs. He left the town of Paucartambo in 1846, crossed the Eastern Andes by the pass of Tres Cruces, and visited the farms of San Miguel and Cosñipata. The results of his researches are embodied in a Report, published at Cuzco in 1846,† in which Colonel Espinar gives a charming description of the scenery of the forests, supplies information respecting the hydrography, and furnishes some account of the three savage tribes of Chunchos, called Huachipayvis, Treyuneris, and Sirineyris.

The next pioneer of discovery in the direction of the Amaru-mayu was the Italian friar, Father Bovo de Revello. He was a man of large proportions, tall and broad-shouldered, with massive forehead, bald head, and long beard. Brave as a lion, foremost to lead in all dangers, he was at the same time gentle and tender-hearted. He had passed several years in the Holy Land, and some time in the missions of Southern Chile. He was well versed in the history of discovery in all parts of the world, was a naturalist, and a good geographer. In 1847 his fervent imagination was fired with the idea of opening a direct route to Europe for the ancient city of Cuzco, the capital of the Yncas. With boundless enthusiasm, ballasted by great learning and scientific knowledge, he plunged into the forests of Paucartambo. He was a true apostle of progress. While he worked for religion, he was also a friend of geographical science. Solitude had for him no terrors, for he found unceasing pleasure in the contemplation of nature, and of man in his wild state. Returning to the old Ynca capital, after a year of close study of his problem in the forests and on the swollen river banks, he published his 'Brillante Porvenir del Cuzco' in 1848, a work remarkable as well for its research and learning, as for its enlightened and practical views. He dedicated it to the good General Medina, then

---

* R. G. S. Journ., vi. p. 174.

† 'Primera Memoria sobres los valles de Paucartambo y adyacentes, por J. D. Espinar.' Cuzco, 1846.

Prefect of Cuzco, and concluded with an ardent appeal to the inhabitants of the Ynca capital. " People of Cuzco," he exclaimed, " to you belongs the initiative for navigating the rivers to the east of your Andes. It is for you, and for your best interests, to turn your backs on the Pacific, and to open up the vast and fertile Amazonian plains."

He then returned to the forests, and when Lieutenant Gibbon, of the U. S. Navy, entered them in 1851, he was accompanied by the enthusiastic Italian missionary to his furthest point, at the junction of the rivers Tono and Piñi-piñi, where the Amaru-mayu may be said to commence.

The appeal of Bovo de Revello to the manhood of the people of Cuzco was not made in vain. He inspired many of them with his own enthusiasm. They formed a " Sociedad Industrial de los Valles de Paucartambo," of which my friend General De la Guarda, then Prefect of Cuzco, became president. Under the lead of a talented young artist, named Manuel Ugalde, thirty-six youths of Cuzco, of the best families, entered the forests, with the intention of attempting the descent of the Amaru-mayu. In 1852 they reached the banks of the Tono, and were joined by Father Bovo de Revello. Ugalde had conceived the idea of utilising the indiarubber of the surrounding forests in the construction of a raft. Search was made for the trees, several depôts were formed, paths were cut through the forests, and eventually a number of indiarubber or waterproof cylinders were prepared, which were secured to the poles forming the raft. Father Bovo de Revello instilled his own enthusiasm into the youth of Cuzco, while Ugalde directed their efforts. Two rafts were thus constructed, and launched at the junction of the Piñi-piñi and Tono. But all these high hopes ended in disappointment. It would seem that they ought to have committed their fortunes to the river below and not above the rapid. In the midst of the impetuous current the raft encountered the rush of a flooded affluent. They were driven on rocks and capsized. Ugalde had taken the precaution to provide life-belts made from the indiarubber he had prepared. His people were all saved; but the expedition, begun with so much promise, and carried through with such forethought and perseverance, was wrecked.

In May 1853, a year after this catastrophe, I penetrated into the forests of Paucartambo.* I found that the Chunchos had since made successful attacks on the few coca and cacao estates, and that only two remained, called San Miguel and Cosñipata. Here I met with Father Bovo de Revello, almost alone. His only food was parched maize, chuñus, and bananas. I went with him to the point where Ugalde commenced his navigation. But he was then destitute of all resources, and enthusiasm alone could not take us further. He was a man of commanding presence. I remember looking upon him as a forlorn hope, holding an outpost against desperate odds. He seemed to feel that while

* See R. G. S. Journ., xxv. p. 151.

he held his ground, like a beacon on a watch-tower, the youths of Cuzco would continue to organise fresh attempts. He was the rallying point. Such a man would not abandon his post while life endured. He died there—a noble martyr to the cause of geographical discovery.

Father Bovo de Revello did not work in vain. He instilled a love of adventure and an ardent desire to achieve success into the people of Cuzco which survived him.

In 1860 Don Faustino Maldonado and seven companions organised a fresh expedition. With scanty means, but full of enthusiasm, they were resolved to encounter and overcome whatsoever dangers and privations might stand in the way rather than fail in their enterprise. The names of these gallant explorers deserve to be held in memory. They were:— Faustino Maldonado, Estevan Trigoso, Andres Guerra, Raimondo Estella, Gregorio Maldonado, Manuel Chapalba, Manuel Santa Rosa, Simon Rodriguez. They left Cuzco on the 26th of December, 1860, descended into the forests, and advanced along the banks of the river Tono, until they reached the junction with the Piñi-piñi. Here they constructed a raft during January 1861, but by the time they had finished it their scanty stock of provisions was exhausted, as well as their ammunition. Most men would have returned. But they resolved to push onwards, trusting to supplies of bananas and yucas from the Indians, or to wild fruit. If these failed they could but die for their country. At all events they would not turn back. This is the stuff that the young men of Cuzco are made of. There are few nobler deeds of heroism recorded in the annals of geographical discovery than the persistency of Maldonado and his comrades in risking all in order that work so important to their fatherland might be done. In February they embarked, and succeeded in navigating their frail raft over the rapids. Next day they were attacked by savages in canoes, who hunted them for many hours. As the days went on they became weak from hunger. Their only food was the bananas occasionally found in clearings along the river banks. Near the mouth of the great river Ynambari they were attacked again, and Andres Guerra was wounded with an arrow. But this was the last hostile act, and soon afterwards they came to a friendly tribe who sold them a canoe. At length they reached the confluence of the Amaru-mayu and Beni, and soon afterwards they approached the rapids near the mouth of the Beni. They had explored the whole course of the Amaru-mayu for the first time since it was descended by the troops of the Ynca Yupanqui in the fifteenth century. It would appear to be a noble stream, and clear of all obstructions from the point of embarkation to the rapids of the Beni. Maldonado and his companions abandoned their raft above the rapids, walked round them, and constructed another below. But they were now very weak and faint from want of food. They proceeded, six of them on the new raft, and two in a small canoe, and on entering the Madeira they met with some friendly Caripuna

Indians, obtaining a little food. Continuing their voyage for several days, the raft got into a dangerous rapid on the 18th of March, was dashed against rocks and broken up. Four out of the six explorers were unfortunately drowned, namely, Maldonado himself, Gregorio Maldonado, Trigoso, and Guerra. Two reached the shore, and the two in the canoe were safe. But the four survivors were nearly naked, weak from fasting, and without food. At length they reached the station of a friendly Brazilian who supplied all their wants. They were sent down to the Brazilian town of Barra, on the Amazons, and returned home by way of Tarapoto in the following May. They had solved one of the two great geographical problems connected with the region to the east of Cuzco. These brave youths of the old Ynca city had explored the whole course of the Amaru-mayu.

In 1865 our Corresponding Member, the accomplished and indefatigable Don Antonio Raimondi, turned his attention to the Paucartambo forests. Like General Miller and Colonel Espinar, Raimondi describes with enthusiasm the magnificent scene which burst on his view from the pass of Tres Cruces. He went to the estate of Cosñipata, but found the labourers in a constant state of alarm at the approach of the savage Chunchos, while all the other estates had been abandoned and destroyed. He returned after making numerous valuable observations.

The next expedition into the Paucartambo forests was undertaken by Juan G. Nystrom in 1868. He reached the confluence of the Piñi-piñi and Tono, reported that the united stream became navigable at the junction of the Marcapata, and fixed several positions by astronomical observations.

The spirit breathed into the people of Cuzco by the enthusiasm of Bovo de Revello, still continued to animate them. In 1873 an expedition was organised consisting of fifty soldiers and pioneers, and commanded by the Prefect of Cuzco himself, Colonel Don Baltazar La Torre. Señor Germain Göhring accompanied the party, to conduct the scientific work. Proceeding by way of Paucartambo and Tres Cruces, the explorers reached Cosñipata on May 25th, and pushed on through the forests, to the junction of the Piñi-piñi and Tono. A few miles further on the united stream forces its way through a chain of hills at a place called Ccoñec, and forms a dangerous rapid. Here Colonel La Torre began the construction of a raft, but there were deluges of rain, and the river rose so that the workmen found themselves on an islet surrounded by the angry flood, and overshadowed by the dense forest. Owing to failure of provisions a number of men were sent back to Cosñipata, and the party was reduced to twenty. At length the raft was finished, and on July 6th it was resolved to move the camp lower down the river. Göhring and four men were to go by land, while the Prefect, his secretary, Don Baldomero Cano, Captain José Maria Chavez, Ensign

Vicente Caloma, and some soldiers embarked on the raft for a trial trip. No sooner was the raft allowed to get into the stream, than it was whirled impetuously along by the current and brought up against an island. All hands, except Colonel La Torre, jumped out to hold it with a rope. But the rope broke, and they beheld their commander, alone on the raft, carried with breathless velocity to the rapids, and disappear amidst the foam and rocks.

They succeeded in wading to the shore, and set out at once in search of the Prefect, but with little hope of ever seeing him alive. Five days afterwards, on July 11th, while they were holding a parley with some Sirineyri Chunchos, a man emerged from the forest, who proved to be their lost commander. He had succeeded in steering the raft safely through the rapids, but she was afterwards wrecked among some rocks. He reached the shore, but had since suffered terrible privations in the forest, and was exhausted with long fasting. The party advanced for another day, and came to a beach with an island in front, where there were about fifty Chunchos. During the night whistling was heard all round them in the woods. Next day, being desirous of establishing friendly relations, Colonel La Torre crossed in a small canoe, to a shingly beach on the island, bordered by forest, with Dr. Cano, young Caloma, and a soldier. The others watched from the river bank. They saw the little party land and make signs, the savages who were standing on the beach suddenly disappeared among the trees, reappeared with bows and arrows, and surrounded the officers. There were shouts, and reports of revolvers, the savages again disappeared in the forest, and all was silent. It was all over in a few minutes. Captain Chavez plunged into the water and swam to the island, followed by four soldiers. They found the body of Colonel La Torre pierced by thirty-four arrows, and with two blows on the head, each sufficient to cause death. Dr. Cano was also dead. Young Caloma had disappeared. Sorrowfully the survivors returned to Cuzco. Göhring had, however, made numerous valuable observations. From a hill he had been able to make out the confluence of the Marcapata with the Amaru-mayu. He constructed a map of the region traversed, and collected 300 mineralogical specimens.

Since the death of La Torre in 1873, we have no further news of the progress of exploration. The calamities which have overtaken Peru, have checked it for a time. The flower of the youth of that country has had to fight desperately for their fatherland. The bones of many young heroes, who might have continued the work of Ugalde and Maldonado, now whiten the deserts of Tarapaca, and form heart-rending piles on the sandhills of Tacna.

There, however, in the ancient capital of the Yncas, is the spirit of enlightened progress still smouldering. The men of Cuzco have worked manfully for geography. They have earned a claim to help from the outer world. Will they not receive it?

We have now passed in review all that has been done to explore the main course of the Amaru-mayu river.

With regard to its principal tributary, the Ynambari, which, deflected by the off-lying range of hills, flows parallel with the Andes, and receives all the streams of Marcapata and Caravaya, our knowledge is still very scanty. The main stream of the Ynambari has never been explored to its junction with the Amaru-mayu ; but its head-waters and most of its tributaries are more or less known. The Marcapata ravines, which come next to the Paucartambo valleys (travelling south and east), have been famous, for the last hundred years, for their auriferous deposits. The golden hill of Camanti was first made known in 1788, and in this century companies have been formed to work it. In 1851 Colonel Bolognesi undertook to collect bark in Marcapata, and while in his employment a young Englishman named Backhouse (son of Mr. Backhouse, of the Foreign Office, who was on our Council from 1836 to 1841) lost his life in an encounter with the Chunchos. Next to Marcapata are the beautiful ravines of Caravaya, also famous for their gold-washings, their coca estates, their coffee and fruit, as well as for their chinchona bark. They have been frequented by traders since the time of the Yncas, and have been the scenes of intelligent enterprises, undertaken by energetic Peruvian capitalists, chief among whom is Don Agustin Aragon. But they have seldom been visited by geographers. In 1864 our Honorary Corresponding Member, Don Antonio Raimondi, communicated to this Society the results of his exploration of the rivers San Gavan and Ayapata ;* and my paper on the province of Caravaya, written after I had visited the ravines of Sandia and of the Huari-huari, was published in our Journal.† Señor Raimondi also made a journey to the gold-mines of Challuma, when he crossed the Huari-huari (Ynambari) river.

With the Huari-huari river, in Caravaya, the Amaru-mayu system comes to an end. It is separated from the basin of the river Beni by a ridge called Marun-kunka ; and the first or most western of the Beni tributaries is the Tambopata.

The lovely ravine of Tambopata, with its sides clothed with many varieties of chinchonaceous trees, foremost among which is the calisaya, was first visited by Dr. Weddell, the eminent quinologist, in 1846, and in 1860 I penetrated for some distance through its dense forests, to a point some miles beyond the Yanamayu tributary. But my duties were not consistent with extended exploration, and Señor Raimondi, in 1864, advanced much further, to a place called Putina-puncu, where the two rivers Tambopata and Pablo-bamba unite, both flowing from the Andes on either side of a lofty forest-covered ridge. Señor Raimondi collected information which convinced him that the Tambopata formed the head-waters of the Madidi, the chief tributary of the Beni. The whole course

---

* Journal, vol. xxxvii. p. 116 (with map).   † Vol. xxxi. p. 190.

of this important river has not yet been explored. All the Andean range, from the Tambopata to Cochabamba, sends feeders to swell the volume of the Beni. Next in importance to the Madidi is the river Mapori, flowing from the bases of the loftiest peaks, Illimani and Illampu, and receiving streams which water the ravine of Tipuani, famous for its gold-washings, and of Coroico, rich in the best species of chinchona trees.

The main stream of the Beni comes from the fertile Yungas of La Paz, and is the future outlet for the trade of the commercial capital of Bolivia.

Until the voyage of Dr. Heath, the course of the Beni had never been completely explored. Searchers for chinchona bark, and searchers for gold, had penetrated far down the ravines leading to it, and in recent years the collectors of indiarubber had gone to still greater distances ; but the most extensive exploration had been achieved by the missionaries. Much of this good work was done by the College of Moquegua, in Peru, established in viceregal times. One of its disciples, Father José Figueira, was in charge of the mission of Cavinas, near the junction of the Beni and Madidi, and in July 1802 he made a voyage on the former river, in the course of which he received distinct information that the Beni united with the Amaru-mayu from Cuzco. A Jesuit mission was established among the Cavinas, near the mouth of the Madidi, in 1827. A missionary named Samuel Mancini was in the basin of the Beni from 1850 to 1864. He actually traversed the region between the Beni and Amaru-mayu, here called the Mayu-tata, reached Sandia in Caravaya, and eventually constructed a map. Colonel Church tells us that two Franciscans whom he knew at La Paz, one named Fidel Codinach, had reached the Amaru-mayu in 1866 by a five days' journey north-west from the mission of Cavinas.

Still the river had never been descended, and the lower and unknown course was so dreaded, that indiarubber collectors actually conveyed all their produce by a roundabout route up the river to avoid it. As regards the mouth of the Beni, in the river Mamoré, an expedition had been sent to ascend its course by the Bolivian Government in 1846, under the command of Don Agustin Palacios. He went up the river for 18 miles, where he found its course obstructed by rocks. Professor Orton, the well-known American explorer, projected the ascent of the Beni in 1877, in company with Mr. Ivon Heath, but his plans were frustrated by a mutiny of his people when within 24 miles of its mouth.

Such was the state of knowledge of this interesting river when Dr. Edwin Heath, brother of Ivon Heath, the companion of Professor Orton, undertook his bold enterprise. Colonel Church truly says that " Dr. Heath is entitled to much praise for his quiet, unobtrusive solution of a problem which has greatly interested the geographical and commercial worlds." Dr. Heath is understood to have been once employed professionally in Peru, in the construction of the Aroya railroad, and

was afterwards similarly employed by the contractors of the Madeira
and Mamoré railway. Thence he entered Bolivia by ascending the
Mamoré to Exaltacion, and proceeded, by the customary route of the
river Yacuma, to Reyes, near the river Beni.

On August 3rd, 1880, Dr. Heath left Reyes to descend the Beni, and
visit the indiarubber camps at Cavinas. He embarked in a boat manned
by eight Indians with paddles. At every bend there is a sand-bar where
animals come from the forest to drink, and in the afternoons jaguars
were often seen. While stopping for breakfast, some of the boatmen
took the opportunity of making themselves new shirts. A young
brazil-nut tree of the proper size was stripped of its bark to a height of
eight or 10 feet. This was taken to the river, placed on a log or stone,
and beaten with a stick. When free from the outer bark the fibres are
opened and form a good cloth. This is then folded in the middle, a
space left for the arms, the sides sewn to near the bottom, and a slit cut
for the head. When old these shirts are as soft as linen; and thus easily
are the boatmen of the Beni supplied with clothing.

At the part of the river reached by Dr. Heath on August 12th, in
latitude 12° 45′ S., there is danger from savage Chuncho Indians who
make incursions every year from the north-west, and kill many of the
peaceful Cavinas, dwellers on the Beni. While at breakfast on the
12th the boatmen hastily covered their fires, quickly and noiselessly
went to their boat, and crossed to the opposite side of the river. They
answered Dr. Heath's inquiry, who was surprised at their evident fear
and caution, by pointing to smoke curling up through the forest near
the camp, and repeating the simple word *barbaros*—savages. Next day
the boat passed the mouth of the Madidi in latitude 12° 33′ 13″ S.; a
great tributary which causes a perceptible increase in the quantity of
water in the river. The mission of Cavinas is two days' pull up the
Madidi.

On the 24th Dr. Heath arrived at Maco in 12° 17′ 25″ S., which is
110 miles from Reyes in a straight line, and 217 from the mouth of the
Beni; but by the river it is 234 miles from Reyes. Here the plague of
sand-flies and mosquitos becomes severe. On this part of the river there
are several indiarubber camps, where the Bolivian collectors are assisted
by families of Pacavara Indians, who make plantations of maize, yuca,
bananas, and sugar-cane. These people pierce the septum of the nose,
and thrust in feathers from each side, at a distance making them look
as if they had huge moustaches. In their ears they wear the eye-teeth
of alligators. Their complexion is almost white, and the women, if
dressed as civilisation requires, would for the most part be beautiful.
They differ from other Amazonian tribes by reason of the rapidity of their
movements and conversation.

On the 19th the boat passed the outlet of a large lake called the
Mamore-bey (from *mamoré*, a fish, and *bey*, a lake), where the *Pirarucu* is

found, and only in this lake, after leaving the falls of San Antonio in Brazil. The banks of the lake are rocky, and in the next bend of the river below it, the rocks jut out, on the south side, nearly to half the width of the river. Rising almost perpendicular above these rocks is a red clay bank 40 feet high. On the 30th Dr. Heath reached a camp where the indiarubber trees were large and numerous, there being over 10,000 trees in a space of five miles square.

Remaining with the indiarubber collectors until September 27th, Dr. Heath then accompanied one of them, Dr. Vaca, down the river. Reaching the camp of Señor Eudara, another rubber collector, his project of continuing the descent of the Beni was encouraged by Mrs. Eudara. When the Pacavara boatmen appeared alarmed at the idea, she said to them " Go with the Doctor, and the Creator will protect you." He continued the voyage in a boat with two Pacavaras. The boat was a most rickety craft, only three fingers' breadth out of the water. On October 6th it was hot and sultry. At 1.10 P.M. a hurricane struck them. Massive trees were wrenched from their sites and hurled many feet; it was a grand spectacle but was over in fifteen minutes.

On October 28th, Dr. Heath arrived at the mouth of the Amaru-mayu, in latitude 10° 51' 42" S. On a sand-bar in the middle there were some *capybaras* wallowing on the edge of the river. They merely raised themselves on their fore-feet, and wondered at the strangers. The Amaru-mayu was here 785 yards wide, the Beni only 243. The depth of the Amaru-mayu, at its shallowest place, was 40 feet. Five miles below, the united stream spreads out to a mile in width, the current running three to five miles an hour.

Only twice had civilised men ever emerged from that Amaru-mayu mouth; the troops of the Ynca Yupanqui in the fifteenth century, and Maldonado with his band of gallant youths of Cuzco in 1866.

Encamping late in the afternoon on a beach, the alligators were found to be numerous and much too familiar. Dr. Heath had found the meat of spider monkeys to be tender and excellent, and, to keep his supply safe, he put it at the head of his bed and partly under his blanket. Towards morning he was awakened by feeling something near him, and soon after heard a plunge into the river. Springing to his feet he found that an alligator had carried off his meat. Looking round he saw a large jaguar not 20 feet from him, which had just dug up a nest of turtle eggs. Having finished them, he marched back into the forest.

On the 9th they met a porpoise. Their absence is an indication of impassable falls, so that this creature was a hopeful sign. The mosquitos now became dense and excessively voracious. At 10 A.M. they came to a rapid, but passed between the rocks with ease. An hour afterwards they were stopped by a line of rocks across the river. On the south side a smooth rock was found, and the boat was drawn over to the waters below which were very turbulent. It was with great difficulty that they prevented the boat from being dashed to pieces. It began to leak badly, necessitating frequent baling. Next day they sighted the hills corresponding to the Palo Grande Fall on the Mamoré, which was already well known to Dr. Heath. He informed the Indians of their position. "Then," said one of them, "there is hope of our not losing our lives. Let us call the fall ‘ Esperanza ’ (Hope) since passing that we have hopes of living." Until that moment he had been under the impression that his days were few and numbered.

Dr. Heath's success had been complete. He had been the first explorer to descend the Beni to its mouth. But he had done much more. He had mapped the whole course of the river with the greatest care, measured widths and depths, calculated volume and velocity of current, and taken astronomical observations. He had achieved an exploit for which he deserves the highest credit; and had done geographical work with care and ability, which is of real importance, in the face of great difficulties.

He determined to return to Bolivia by ascending the Mamoré to Exaltacion, a distance of 325 miles. Thence he took the route by the river Yacuma, and once more arrived at Reyes by the 11th of December. He received a fitting reception. Bells were rung, houses decorated, a holiday proclaimed, school children met him outside and escorted him into the town, and there was a special mass. All the people seemed to consider his work as a public benefit.

Dr. Heath's descent of the Beni has given an extraordinary stimulus to the indiarubber trade. Previously 185 men were engaged in collecting on the Beni, who gathered 104,000 lbs. in 1880. Within four months after his return to Reyes there were 644 men engaged, and now there are probably many more. When the Beni and Amaru-mayu are opened for commerce, the yield of indiarubber will be enormous, for all the vast plains are covered with the trees. Coffee, cacao, brazil-nuts, formerly only collected for home use, will be largely exported. Vanilla beans used to be left to rot on the trees. Ipecacuanha, cinnamon, copaiba, matico abound, but never were collected for want of the means of export. This is the region of the chinchona bark richest in quinine. Hides, deer, jaguar, and sloth skins would also be articles of export. This region, too, is the home of the cardenal, of several species of *crax* and *penelope*, of the curassow, of the ant-bear, armadillo, peccary, tapir, and several kinds of monkeys.

In April, Dr. Heath again left Reyes, and ascended the whole course of the river of La Paz, reaching the city of La Paz on July 25th, 1882.

We have now passed in review the efforts which have been made to explore these two great rivers, the Amaru-mayu forming an outlet for the Peruvian city of Cuzco, and the Beni forming an outlet for the Bolivian city of La Paz. Both have been navigated to their mouths once and only once; the Amaru-mayu by Maldonado and the young

Peruvian explorers in 1866, the Beni by Dr. Heath in 1881. Both need further examination, and many important parts of the splendid region which they drain are still unknown. We want an accurate description of the great lake of Rogoaguado. The courses of the Madidi and of the Ynambari remain to be discovered, and of many other great rivers. Here then is a magnificent field for the explorer, as interesting geographically and historically, as it is important from a commercial point of view. There should be a helping hand to the gallant men of Cuzco, the ancient capital of the Yncas, to realise the brilliant dreams of Bovo de Revello. There should be willing aid to the people of La Paz, to the dwellers round the sacred lake, to open their hitherto closed up doors and let in the light of civilising commerce.

In no part of the world can the exploring geographer find a nobler field for his exertions than on the grand rivers which traverse the virgin . forests of the Yncas.

Exploration of the River Beni in 1880-1. By EDWIN R. HEATH, M.D.

Map, p. 376.*

IN 1869 or 1870 reports coming from Cavinas that the indiarubber tree grew in that place, two Bolivians, Francisco Cardinas and Pablo Salinas, went there and obtained specimens of the rubber, which they sent to Europe. The quality proving excellent, a few men entered into the business of rubber-gathering, but confined their operations to the region about Cavinas.

On arriving at Reyes, near the river Beni, I could obtain very little information regarding the river I hoped to descend. Ten months' residence at Reyes only made the undertaking appear next to impossible. An opportunity presenting of visiting the indiarubber camps at Cavinas, I left Reyes on August 3rd, 1880, for the river Beni, distant 12 miles.

The first league was open prairie, then came nine miles of dense forest, with mud six to eighteen inches deep. The carts had been sent early on the morning of the 2nd, arriving the evening of the 4th. These carts returning carried rubber, but required four days to reach Reyes. There the rubber is sewed up in hides in packages of 150 to 200 lbs. It is then transported in carts to the river Yacuma 57 miles, then in boats to Santa Ana, and other boats down the Mamoré and Madeira rivers to San Antonio, Brazil, where the monthly Amazons steamers receive it and deliver it to the rubber houses at Para. The time required to transport the rubber from the camps at Cavinas to the port

---

* This map is from Dr. Heath's own reduction of his surveys. Copies of his large-scale survey maps of the river, made from the originals lent to us for the purpose, are deposited in the map-room of the Society. The reduced map can only be considered as provisional, until the whole of Dr. Heath's great survey can be published on a scale large enough to show the detail of the rivers.

of Reyes varies from 25 to 50 days. One can realise what dread there must have been of the unknown course of the river lower down, to cause such a circuit and loss of time. Reference to the map will assist one in realising this condition of the trade routes in August 1880.

On the 6th, the boat being loaded at 10 A.M. the eight Indians dipped their paddles, and the voyage down the Beni commenced. At 4.17 P.M. the mouth of the small stream Seyuba was passed, and camp was made soon after on a sand-bar in front. The Seyuba rises in mountains at Tumupasa, and the Tacana Indians living there follow it to its mouth, in their yearly visit to the Beni, to fish and collect turtle eggs on the sand-bars. Their indications of the position of the town of Tumupasa, with the mouth of the Seyuba, gave me my first idea regarding the error of the geographical position of that town.

The day had become overcast, and at 8 P.M. the wind suddenly changed from north-west to the south, blowing with great violence. At 9 P.M. the rain began to pour; towards morning it turned to drizzle, with a stiff breeze; the thermometer fell from 94° to 62° Fahr. The 7th of August was passed under shelter. On the 8th, although it still rained at times and the thermometer stood at 62°, orders were given to advance, and the Indians taking off their only covering, a bark shirt, took their paddles, shivering with cold. At 2·45 P.M. the mouth of the little river Tarene, emptying into the Beni from the west, was passed. Its mouth represents the port of the town of Ysiamas. During the afternoon various jaguars were seen on the sand-bars, and camping at 6 P.M. the ground was found covered with their footprints. August 9th, the river and its bends became wider, with a current of one to two miles per hour.

10th.—At 7 A.M. the river Enaporera was passed, at 8.56 A.M. the Tequeje, and at 2.20 P.M. the Undumo. These streams, 30 to 50 feet wide at low water and 8 to 10 feet deep, empty into the Beni from the west. The night being favourable, an observation for latitude was made, using a triangle Aust., giving 13° 12′ 15″ S. lat.; the lower part of Reyes being in S. lat. 14° 15′ 56″.

11th.—Many jaguars seen to-day. At 4.2 P.M. stopped in the mouth of the river Negro. It was 100 feet wide, 20 feet deep, without current at its mouth. This river had been partly ascended by a Frenchman, who reported the alligators so vicious that he had to return. There being no good place to camp, the descent was continued until 5.3 P.M. The clouds prevented an observation.

12th.—While at breakfast the Indians hastily covered their fires, quickly and noiselessly went to their boat, and immediately crossed to the other side of the river. Surprised at this evident fear and caution, they answered our inquiry as to the cause by pointing to smoke curling up through the forest near our camp and saying the simple but expressive word *barbaros*, their word for savages. We learned afterwards that every year this region is visited by a savage and warlike tribe of cannibals, who live in the north-west, and who kill many of the Cavinas Indians. Current two miles per hour. Camped in S. lat. 12° 45′ 27″.

13th.—Killed three large spider monkeys, called by the natives *marimonos*. A large fire being made they were thrown in the flames, which singed their hair and blistered the skin, making it easy to clean off. When scraped they appear like naked white children. An elevated platform of green poles is made over embers, and the monkeys placed entire upon them, where they are roasted. The food is rich, and preferable to all others as soon as one learns to forget their resemblance to human beings.

Early in the morning we passed the little brook called Santa Clara, the old port for the mission of Cavinas. The next bend below has a high red bank, the first high land since leaving Reyes. In former years, a tribe of Guarayo Indians had a village on this high ground. They are now extinct or moved to other parts. At 12.22 P.M. we passed the arroya Vira. About 4 P.M. the river being very low exposed some rocks and made a strong current, needing care to pass. At 4 P.M. stopped at Santa Rosa, the first place where rubber was collected, now deserted for better places below. At 5.15 passed the mouth of the river Madidi in S. lat. 12° 33′ 13″. This is the first important tributary of the lower Beni and causes a perceptible increase in the quantity of the water in the river. Two days' rowing up the Madidi brings one to the mission of Cavinas.

14th.—Passed Todos Santos and San Antonio, arriving at our destination, Maco, at 2.8 P.M. in S. lat. 12° 17′ 25·5″, distant in right line 110 miles from Reyes, 117 miles from port of Reyes, 217 miles from the mouth of the Beni. Distant by river from the port of Reyes 234 miles. Time of descent, 58 hours and 30 minutes. I had the good fortune to find the proprietor of Maco ready with boats and men to descend the Beni in search of a new rubber place. Accepting a place in his boat my voyage was resumed on the 16th. At 1.8 P.M. we stopped to take coffee at Sinosino, and camped for the night at San José, another rubber camp in S. lat. 12° 07′ 33″. The bank of Sinosino was nearly 50 feet above the river. The river from Maco begins now to gain direction eastward. Sand-flies, *maruins*, and *tabanos*, black and yellow, make the days intolerable, while the mosquitos by night give no rest.

17th.—We passed San Juan, Santo Domingo, California, Etea, San Lorenzo, camping at 12.30 A.M. on the 18th at Santa Ana, the last rubber camp. Here we found a family of Pacavara Indians who were living with Don Fidel Endara and helping him to collect rubber and make plantations of rice, corn, yuca, bananas, sugar-cane, and build houses. Both men and women pierce the septum of the nose through which they thrust feathers from each side, at a distance making them appear as having heavy mustachios. They wear in their ears the eye-teeth of alligators. Their complexion is almost white, and the females, if dressed as civilisation requires, would be for the most part beauties. Their movements and conversation are rapid, differing from all other Amazonian tribes I ever met. Their mode of counting is by closing the hands, and as each finger is opened, saying *nata*. When the ten fingers are finished they say *echasu*. Needing more numbers, they repeat *nata* with each toe, and again repeat *echasu* at the close. Thus using fingers and toes they continue until the number is reached.

18th.—At 2.20 P.M. we resumed our march, Don Fidel Eudara accompanying us, having two Pacavara Indians as part of his crew. Camped on a sand-bar near the mouth of the Jenejoya river.

19th.—Passed the Jenejoya, a river 200 feet wide and 20 feet deep. About six miles up this river is the village of the Pacavara Indians.

About 10 A.M. we passed an *arroya* (little stream), the outlet of a large lake called by the Indians Mamoreboy, from *mamore*, a fish, and *bey*, a lake, the *Pirarucu* being found there and only there on the Beni. The banks on the north side at Mamoreboy are rocky, and on the south side, the next bend below, the rocks jut out nearly to half the width of the river. Rising almost perpendicularly above these rocks is a red clay bank 40 feet high. On an island, two bends below the clay bank, we saw a number of capybaras feeding. We succeeded in killing one. More than half the weight of the living animal is water, and the meat is unpalatable till dried.

21st.—We advanced a little, remaining in our new camp till the 23rd. Señor Vasquez, whose guest I was, resolved to remain at this point. After much persuasion, I succeeded in getting a boat with nine Indians placed at my service. Accompanied by two Bolivians, we resumed our descent.

24th.—At 11.35 A.M. we passed the Jeneshuaya, a river equal in size to the Jenejoya. From this point our Pacavara Indians gave indications of fear to go any further down the river, and this fear communicated itself to my companions.

25th.—After advancing slowly all day we camped at 5.43 P.M., the Indians refusing to advance further. This was in S. lat. 11° 11' 29", 47 hours 16 minutes actual voyage from Maco. My calculations gave the mouth of the Beni as being 143 miles distant in a right line. Pleading did no good, and on August 26th we began to retrace our course up stream, reaching on the 30th unexpectedly a large clearing, where we found Señor Vasquez. He called his new place "Concepcion." The rubber trees here were large and numerous, there being more than 10,000 trees in a space of five miles square. On the 12th of September we again arrived at Maco.

On the 21st three of us started, opposite Maco, to cut our way through the forest on the south bank as far as the pampas. We began at 6 A.M., each taking the lead in turn, and cutting vines and underbush till we were tired. In four hours we reached the open pampas, but it took us only fifteen minutes to return. This will convey some little idea of travel through the Amazons forest.

I ascended the river a few days afterwards to San Antonio, and there met nineteen Arauna Indians, who lived on the Madre de Dios, north and west of San Antonio. These Indians do not pierce their ears and nose. Small of stature, ugly featured, one could readily believe them to be cannibals. Three years previous, Dr. Vaca, owner of San Antonio, had purchased a boy of this tribe, who now speaks Spanish and serves as interpreter. Through him, as interpreter, we learned they considered the descent of the Beni to its mouth impossible. Dr. Vaca, I found, had provisioned boats, and sent them down the river to select sites for new rubber camps, and afterwards to descend ten days' journey beyond the furthest point I had reached on my former attempt. Dr. Vaca himself was going to follow, on a visit to his rubber station called California, where he had a small boat which he would let me have for my voyage down the river. I was not long in determining to join his party. On the 27th of September, with Dr. Vaca and nine Arauna Indians, in addition to our native crew, we began the downward voyage. Don Antenor Vasquez sent with me one of his Indians, one who had been my body servant on my last voyage. He, the Indian, volunteered to go with me, even though every one tried to dissuade him.

Sept. 28th.—We landed at California. There I found submerged an old boat 15 feet long by 4 feet wide. Bow and stern I could thrust my hand through. Pulling it on land we caulked it as well as we could with corn husks, and plastered mud over them. In this I was resolved to complete the exploration of the Beni. Hastily collecting a few things necessary, we were soon ready to start. The Mobima Indian assigned to go with me and the Indian of Señor Vasquez, was suddenly taken sick, whereon Dr. Vaca ordered another man to take his place. We pushed into the stream the gunwale of our boat one inch only out of water. The boat leaked so badly we were obliged to bale constantly, and it was very doubtful if we should reach the next camp. At 5.50 p.m. we tied up at the camp of Juan Limpias. There we unloaded, and with nails, bark, and mud, repaired our boat. The next day, on launching, it was found dry and good.

29th.—We arrived at Santa Ana and were welcomed by Señor Eudara and the Pacavara Indians. When they comprehended what I proposed doing the Pacavara appeared frightened. They had formerly told me, Señora Eudara serving as interpreter (she having learned to converse with them) that savage Indians inhabited the lower Beni, and advised me to shoot at sight any Indian with long hair. Señora Eudara was the only person in Bolivia who did not throw cold water on the undertaking. She told my two Indians to " go with the Doctor and the Creator would protect them." As we cast off to continue our advance, the Pacavaras, men and women, stood on the bank and murmured "death, death." I afterwards learned that they put on mourning for a month to counteract the evil effects of having looked upon the dead.

30th.—Came suddenly upon the camp at Mamorebey of the boats sent by Dr. Vaca. They had descended to the river Jeneshuaya, made a clearing, planted bananas, and were on their return, indignant at the presumption of Dr. Vaca in sending them to die. Satisfied that I could not persuade them to continue with me, I resolved to go ahead with my two Indians. I was then informed that one of these Indians belonged to Dr. Vaca, and I had to give him up. My other Indian, Ildefonzo Roca, had a raging fever; I told him how matters stood, and asked him if he would return with these men to Maco; he answered "No; I am going with you as far as you go." Procuring some provisions, as soon as Ildefonzo was a little better, we went down the bank to our boat. It was then that Dr. Vaca's agent consented to let the other Indian go also. As we started our boat had only three fingers' breadth out of water.

October 1st.—At 5 P.M. we reached Concepcion, and remained here during the 2nd and 3rd, Ildefonzo being sick.

4th.—My Indian being a little better we resumed our journey. At 10 A.M. his fever returned, and we had to tie up. The heat, sandflies, tabanos, and the sickness of my best man made the prospects of our expedition look doubtful, but did not cause one moment's hesitation to proceed.

5th.—We resumed our voyage, I taking the paddle of Ildefonzo, who lay still in the boat. About 4 P.M. met the canoe of one of the rubber-gatherers who had gone down to a place near the river Jeneshuaya. I took this opportunity of offering my men their freedom to return. This they refused to do, and we bade good-bye to civilisation for many days.

6th was a very hot sultry day. At 1.10 P.M. a hurricane struck us. Massive trees were wrenched from their roots and hurled many hundred feet distant. It lasted only fifteen minutes but was grand in its might and effects. The cool air aided us all and for the first time Ildefonzo took his paddle in earnest.

7th.—At midday we passed the last point reached on our former descent. Various times each day we landed to explore the country and see if there were any indications of hostile Indians. We camped on a sand-bar in mid-river in lat. 11° 04' 46·2".

The 8th found us again advancing. At 8 A.M. we saw a stream emptying in from the south similar to the Jenejoya, to which I gave the name Ivon, in memory of Ivon D. Heath, the companion of the late Professor James Orton. At 12 A.M. we found ourselves at the junction of a much larger stream, the Madre de Dios. Triangulation gave it 2350 feet wide and the lesser stream 735 feet wide. Having met with a large island two bends above with similar appearances, we had left the Beni proper before we realised it, and then it was too late to return and

measure the depth of the Beni. The Madre de Dios was 40 feet deep
at its shallowest places. Some five miles below, the river spreads out
to a mile in width. The current is now three to five miles an hour.
We camped at 4.30 P.M.; alligators abundant and very friendly.
Lat. 10° 51′ 42·2″; sat up till nearly 2 A.M. to get an observation.
Having had our monkey meat taken from our boat every night by the
alligators, I took the precaution of putting the meat at the head of my
bed and partly under the blanket. Towards morning I was awakened
by feeling something near me, then soon after heard a plunge in the
river. Springing to my feet, I found an alligator had carried off
our meat. Occupied by this event I did not notice at first a large
jaguar not 20 feet away who had just dug up a nest of turtle eggs.
Having finished his eggs he marched into the forest. All animals
being so tame led me to hope for a safe passage.

9th.—At 6 A.M. we passed a large stream empting from the north.
To this I gave the name Orton. This river is as large as the Madidi.
At 12.15 P.M. saw a porpoise; a fresh-water species very common in the
Amazons, Madeira, Mamoré, and Yacuma rivers. Their absence from
the Beni has been considered proof positive of impassable falls above its
junction with the Madeira. This lonely creature kept us company all
day and part of the next. It gave me great hope of success.

Sunday, 10th.—Passed two large islands ; the tabano flies left us. At
10 A.M. we arrived at a rapid, but passed between the rocks with ease.
At 11 A.M. we were stopped by a line of rocks crossing the river. Land-
ing on the north side of the main fall, and climbing a high point, I
studied the situation : Can we pass? on this side no, unless we draw our
boat overland through the forest ; with but one knife this was not to be
thought of. Crossing to the south side we found a smooth rock, and
over that finally drew our boat to the waters below. With great difficulty
we prevented our boat from being dashed to pieces by the turbulent
waters below. At 6 P.M. we were loaded, and started to pass through
the waves raised by the fall; our boat nearly filled. As darkness
settled down we tied beside the bank, where a ledge some two feet wide
gave sleeping room for my two Indians. I passed the night alternately
bailing and inking over my notes and perfecting my map. The hard
usage had made the boat leak badly; I had to bale often. This was a
night to be remembered; although very tired after paddling 10 hours
and working like a servant, I had yet no time to sleep.

As soon as we could see we started on the 11th without breakfast or
supper the night previous. About 8 A.M. I recognised the hills that
correspond to Palo Grande fall on the river Mamoré, and turning to my
Indians I informed them of our position and positive success. This is
the point where Bursa in 1846 reported finding so many savages. At
10 A.M. we landed at the mouth of the Beni, at a banana patch planted
August 20th, 1879, while ascending into Bolivia.

Our success had been complete. What should we do now? To
return by the Beni would be hazardous in case of sickness or accident;
therefore we decided to ascend the Mamoré 325 miles to Exaltacion.
By this time our food had been reduced to what game we could procure,
dried plantains and yuca (now wormy), and yuca meal. To prevent
the loss of my notes in case of accident, I wrote out a condensed
account, directed it to the owner of the plantation, which I placed in a
safe place, and I cut a notice of it in a tree. While stopping for dinner,
I again cut in a tree notice of what had been done. That night we
slept at the foot of the rapid Lages.

The 12*th* was passed in the same place owing to sickness of one of
my men. On the 13th we passed Lages and Palo Grande rapids. At
the latter we had our boat submerged, losing all our bananas, rubber
clothing, and our last knife; our food, which was sewed up in a hide,
and our paddles were carried to the centre of an immense whirlpool,
and were saved by swimming to them and pushing them out—one of
our paddles was lost. Finding a stick that had once been blocked out
to make a paddle, I patiently reduced it to the proper size by aid of fire
and a stone.

15*th*.—We passed the falls of Banancira, which corresponds to
"Esperanza" on the Beni. ·

16*th*.—We passed the rapids of Guajara-Guassu and Guajara-Merim.

17*th*.—Being a windy and stormy day we had to tie up most of the
time, the waves being too high for our boat. That night, about 10 P.M.,
I was obliged to call my Indians, who were sleeping on the bank near
by. We had barely time to take our things out, as the boat filled and
sank.

18*th*.—After an hour of hard work we succeeded in causing our boat
to float. It leaked badly, and until November 5th when we arrived at
the port of San Martin, the lower port for Exaltacion, my feet were not
dry, and it was with great care we kept afloat. S. lat. 10° 09' 45".

We left Exaltacion on the 10th of November, and resumed our
ascent of the Mamoré, finally reaching Reyes on the 11th of December.
On our arrival bells were rung, houses decorated, a holiday proclaimed,
school children met me three miles out and escorted me to Reyes,
mass was said, and all seemed to consider my work as a public benefit.
Men became crazed over the rubber prospect, and many sold their
cattle and lands to go into the business. Before the exploration, 185
men were engaged in collecting rubber on the river Beni, gathering
104,000 lbs. in 1880. Within four months after the exploration that
number had increased to 644, and most likely by this time there are from
1000 to 2000 employed. What then must the yield be now? They
then only gathered eight months each year, needing the remainder to
deliver the rubber at the port of Reyes, to plant their rice, yuca,
bananas, corn, onions, &c., and collect palm-nuts. Now they only lose

two months in the working of their plantations, having ten months to employ in collecting rubber. Formerly, coffee, cacao, and brazil nuts were only collected for home use, now they can be exported in large quantities. Vanilla beans were left to rot on the vines. Ipecac, copaiba, cinnamon, coto bark, matico, were never gathered. Hides, deer, tiger, and sloth skins were occasionally shipped. This is the home of the cardenal, matico, tordo curiche, tordo birds; wild turkeys, mutun or currasow turkey, jacumin ostrich, the ant-bear, armadillo, wild hog, and various species of monkeys. The *Victoria Regia*, and numerous varieties of the passion flower are abundant.

ASCENT OF THE BENI AND LA PAZ RIVERS.

April 26th, 1882.—Having, as already narrated, descended the Beni from near Reyes to its mouth, I now set out to navigate the upper river as far as the city of La Paz. I left Reyes, accompanied by Mr. Fetterman and his Bolivian wife. We arrived at Rurinabaque, the upper port of Reyes, on the Beni, that night. The port is 24 miles from Reyes by the road, the last 20 miles being through dense forests. Although the main road between the department of Beni and Lake Titicaca, by way of Apolobamba, it is in a very bad state. Between this port and the lower one, called Port of Salinas, or Cavinas, there are three rapid places, and for this reason all rubber from below used to be left at the lower port. That no part of the river might be omitted in my map, I started on April 28th with a canoe and six Indians to visit the lower port. The descent was made in three hours. As we passed the third current I pointed out the place where the raft of Cura Scratia overturned, which mishap cooled his zeal for the further continuance of the exploration. Working early and late, we succeeded in returning by midday on the 30th.

May 2nd and 3rd I occupied in going on mule-back to Tumupasa, which I found in S. lat. 14° 07' 48", and San José directly west of this on the river Teuché. The correct positions of Tumupasa, San José, and Ysiamas were determined. Tumupasa is on the side of the Andine chain just above the forests, so that looking eastward one sees only a sea of verdure. To reach San José it is necessary to pass one mountain and descend to the valley beneath. Ysiamas is situated in the forest at the foot of and away from the mountains. Opposite Rurinabaque, on the west side of the river Beni, is a little town, called San Buenaventura. Between this town and Tumupasa, there are fifty-three streams to cross of various sizes. The large ones only are noted on my map. From Rurinabaque, the upper Beni is traversed by rafts made from the *balsa* tree (*Ochroma piscatoria*). These rafts are made by nailing seven logs together by means of strips of black palm. The logs are five to eight inches in diameter. The rafts are from 25 to 30 feet long, and five to seven feet wide. These are cut slanting to a point in front. The logs are chosen with a curve so that the extreme bow shall be some two feet elevated, thus preventing the submerging of the front as it touches a current or fall. Into the fifth and fourth logs, counting from the centre, strips of black palm are nailed so that their top is one foot above the raft. Midway between these palm sticks stiff poles are lashed across the raft, and upon them a floor of slit bamboo placed and fastened with strips of bark. The same is done to the upper part of the palm sticks; this forms an elevated platform with sides for the baggage and passengers. This platform is called *huaracha*. Two cords of twisted bark the size of a bed cord and 50 feet long, are tied to the bow, and a bit of board six inches long is set in lengthwise and lashed tightly, as a rest for a pole when towing, the Indian *balsero* by this means keeping the raft from the shore. Three men are necessary to manage a raft, two in front and one behind. Each is provided with a pole 18 feet long and a paddle. The raft is poled up stream or towed when sand-bars or the shore permits, and the paddle is used in crossing from side to side as necessity demands.

15th.—We loaded and started, having only four balsas and scant number of men. Passing through the narrow "Encañada," a gorge made by a crossing spur of the Andes, we began towing along a sand-bar, but soon camped and rearranged our rafts.

16th.—We resumed our ascent in earnest, and passing another narrow gorge through a mountain that has a small hole through it near the top, as if pierced by a cannon ball, from which it derives the name Encañada de Bala, we camped at the mouth of the river Sanis in S. lat. 14° 34' 51'. Up the stream were a party of men collecting peruvian bark.

17th.—Early in the day we passed the mouth of the river Tuichi in estimated lat. S. 14° 36' 51", Rurinabaque being in 14° 26' 21", and Tumupasa 14° 07' 48". My map is correct, though differing from all others. Just below the junction the river is cut up with islands, the western side being a yellow clay bank 70 feet high, and the current very swift. During the afternoon we passed the mouth of the river Quiquibey, and camped just above.

18th.—Our progress to-day was very slow, as the river spreads very much and is full of large islands, the river Apichana emptying in on the west. Towards evening we saw in front of us the appearance of five gable ends of the roofs of houses. They were the ends of mountains now nearly perpendicular, made so by the river during high water. We camped just above them. Our rain-gauge indicated 2·756 inch to-day. During the night the river rose so as to float our rafts from the sand-bar where they were drawn, it being necessary to draw the rafts out of water every night to prevent the logs becoming water soaked.

May 19th was passed struggling amidst the islands and currents. Being obliged to cross the river where it was wide, rapid, and deep, one of our rafts, carrying the provisions, struck a snag and upset. Everything being securely lashed to the huaracha, and the raft finally brought to shore, we found ourselves deprived of all our sugar and bread, the former dissolved and washed away, the latter soaked and spoiled. A cage full of small parrots was washed away and lost.

20*th*.—We passed the river Sihuapio, and camped at the base of a spur of mountains that here crossing the river, follow down the river, on the east side and then jut out north-east into the pampas, their cut-off ends forming the gable ends referred to as passed May 18th.

21*st*.—Was a perilous day for all. The river was narrow with several precipices 400 feet high, perpendicular to the river. This is called the Encañada de Veo, and at one place where an island obstructs the river, making a difference of level of two feet, there is a fall. This forms an impassable limit to steam navigation on the river so long as the obstruction is not removed. The little streams Sipita and Sama empty in this narrow gorge.

22*nd*.—Opened rainy, and poured all day, with a south wind and thermometer down to 62°. At about 11 A.M. we ascended the river Quendeque (Indian name Tutiquo) to the junction of the river Chapi. There we met some peruvian bark collectors encamped, who received us kindly. Four days' raft travelling up the Quendeque brings you to a point within two and one-half days of Apolobamba by mules.

23*rd*.—The rain having ceased, we descended the Quendeque, and again began the ascent of the Beni. The river having risen some four feet made the current very strong and the labour of our balseros very heavy.

24*th*.—River fell 2½ feet during the night. Early in the morning we crossed the mouth of the river named Caca, on the maps, but called there Huanai. This river is formed by the junction of the rivers Mapiri and Tipuhuani. The river Mapiri has beside it a large plantation of peruvian bark trees, Otto Richter, of La Paz, having one million trees. The river Tipuhuani is celebrated for its gold-mines (placer mines). We camped at the post of the Muchanes Mission, S. lat. 15° 10' 08". Fraile Padre Louis Fernandez, Padre Prefect of this mission, has a fine place here where he instructs the Mositana Indians. Our reception was very cordial. His care is over the two missions, Santa Ana and Covendo above, and Tumupasa, San José, Ysiamas, San Buenaventura and Cavinas below.

25*th* and 26*th*.—The river hereabout has few islands, less current, and the mountain chains on each side are separated from each other by a distance of about six miles, the river zigzaging from one chain to the other. Passing the river Iniqua we camped at the little collection of bark-collectors' huts, to which they give the name Iniqua.

27*th*.—Found one of our best men this morning with tetanus, the result of exposure during the rain and cold after the great fatigue of the passage of the Encañada de Veo. At 8 P.M. he died.

28th.—About noon we left Iniqua ; at the same time a collector of bark, who had accompanied us from San Buenaventura, having fastened side by side two balsas, forming a *callapo*, started down the river. He assured me he would arrive in three days, although we had occupied eleven in the ascent. Another spur of mountains here cross the Beni, forming the Encañada de Iniqua. We camped at the mouth of the little stream Misere in S. lat. 15° 22' 29". Leaving this gorge, the river forms a succession of rapids, having two to ten feet fall, in short distances, and then long stretches of river with little current. Thus we passed May 29th and 30th, arriving at 12 A.M. of the 30th at the mission of Santa Ana. Fraile Padre Cesario Fernandez received us with open arms. He took great interest in my maps, and showed a map he had made, which, for one not skilled in the use of the sextant and compass, was a marvel of accuracy; it represented all the localities of the various Indian tribes in Eastern Bolivia and Peru. To cheer our men I paid for a mass, to hear which, early on the 31st we were summoned by the tones of the church bell. The choir were all Mositana Indians, and their instruments—violins, harp, bajones (made of palm leaves, and giving as fine a bass tone as any reed organ), flutes—were made by themselves, and a more solemn and better mass I never witnessed, even though I had often attended the 28th-Street Cathedral in New York city while a medical student. Having spent all the night in fruitless watching for break in the clouds for an observation, I had the satisfaction of a meridian altitude of the sun, which gave S. lat. 15° 30' 36". As the Padre and his Indians had often visited Reyes, I was glad to get them to examine and criticise my map, which they did thoroughly bend by bend, and after two hours' careful study told me that it lacked nothing and could not be changed or corrected in any part. The Indians asked the Padre how it was possible that any one passing but once over the ground could be so exact. Above Santa Ana there are many islands, and the river spreads out foaming, becoming more rapid in its current.

June 1st.—We camped at Chevoy, a collection of huts of the bark collectors, and June 2nd at Huachi, another similar collection. Here we spent June 3rd, 4th, 5th, drying our balsas clothing and resting our men. Huachi is in lat. S. 15° 39' 25", 1422 feet above sea-level; estimated distance from Reyes by river 325 miles, with descent of 662 feet, making an average of two feet per mile; while Reyes, distant 2000 miles from the Atlantic by river, having 760 feet elevation, has but ·38 of a foot per mile. This would be the end of steam navigation after removing the obstruction at the Encañada de Veo, which I have before mentioned. Just above Huachi, the Beni river begins by the junction of the rivers from La Paz and Cochabamba. Railroads could easily be built to those two cities following these streams. A short distance above the junction on the river from Cochabamba is the mission of Covendo. The ascent of the Rio de La Paz, or Bopi, was now before us with its discomforts and dangers.

6th.—At midday we left Huachi. Scarcely had we ascended the Bopi two miles, having risen 73 feet, when a sharp current nearly upset one of our balsas.

7th.—We passed the two bad passes of Santa Felicidad (unloading we carried our freight some 300 feet) and Juan de Lana. We stopped to breakfast where the river Cincollachi empties into the Bopi, and where we met bark-gatherers. At night we camped at the foot of the *mal paso* of Tres Bancos. A peculiar botanical division of peruvian bark exists here. Up the ravine of the river from Cochabamba the outer part of the cinchona trees is green in colour, but passing the crest, west of that, it is red.

8th.—We passed the Tres Bancos *mal paso Chico* No. 1 and 2, and arrived about noon at an island where a continuous succession of dangerous rapids called mal pasos obliged the unloading of everything and passing the balsas up the rapids, and loading again above. We were all obliged to walk nearly a mile and a half through the rain, crossing both outlets of the river Chispani. At the residence of a bark-collector we passed the night. The lofty mountains close in upon the river, so that there are but six hours of daylight.

9th.—We passed the rapid Santa Rosa, the mal paso Ayuna, where there is 15 feet fall in 300 feet of distance, and camped on some rocks, wet and tired, to pass a tedious night, it beginning to rain at 7 P.M. and continuing all night. Unrefreshed we resumed our journey.

10th.—We soon passed the river Lerco and mal paso of that name, then Huichini, Huayreruni mal pasos, and at the latter unloaded everything, and with great difficulty passing the rafts. At Chunchu muerto (dead Indian) mal paso the men have to pass the rafts singly up a current some 400 feet long. My raft being last, I had the pleasure of seeing a balsa and two Indians descend this rapid. Naked, with only a handkerchief for breechcloth, with paddle in hand, partly crouching, they awaited each movement of their rafts, and a dip here and there guided it safely where one little false stroke or one unguarded movement would be fatal. These two men turned their raft beside mine and handed me a letter. News having been carried ahead by a man that had left Huachi the day after our arrival, a sick bark-collector had sent these men after me. Leaving my raft and mounting their light unloaded one, I quickly passed the other rafts, and began the ascent of the mal paso Chico, where there is a fall of 25 feet in 200. Our rafts passed the night just above this, while I on foot passed the mal paso of San Fernando, wading the stream of that name. The mal paso of San Fernando is a fall of 8 feet in 20 with a large cutting the channel there narrowed, by projecting mountains on each side, into two parts. I arrived at 6 P.M. at Porto Rico, the residence of the invalid. An acute attack of rheumatism from exposure was causing him suffering and fear of fatal results, common to these men. His wife was afflicted with a thickened cornea, a disease very frequently met with in the mountains of Eastern Bolivia. At 2 P.M. our rafts arrived, and men exhausted with overwork and poor food.

12th.—We advanced a little, and on the 13th we arrived at Siguani, the residence of Señor Cardinas, the owner of the rafts, and with whom we had contracted to carry us to Miguillo, the head of balsa navigation. Here we remained resting and drying our boxes till the 17th. From just below Porto Rico to Siguani, the river bed is wider and the mountains more separated. Just above Siguani they again close in on the river.

18th.—We passed the river Chaquitas with its bark huts, and San José, and breakfasted at the foot of Charia mal paso. Here we were obliged to carry everything a distance of 1500 feet. Then we passed Santa Rosa Foriati, Mono-muerto rapids, the river Evenai and its house, and camped at La Asunta, a little village of bark-collectors, in lat. 16° 7′ 16″ S. We have now left behind us the Amazonian forest, and the mountain tops are less densely covered with vegetation. The valley here is wide and open. Across the river is La Asunta de Belmonte, where Señor Belmonte has a large village of his workmen, and plantations of peruvian bark trees. An American, Dr. Gove, lives here during the dry season while working the gold-mines on the river Cajones, a short distance above.

19th.—We passed the river Cajones, and afterwards the Quinuni, just beyond which the river runs west and east. We camped at Charabamba. Colton's map represents this as a town, and so it was a few years ago; but being composed of bark-collectors, and the bark having given out, all left—except the great percentage who accepted residences underground. We found only one little hut here. The difficulties of the passes above made it necessary that we should leave here a part of our baggage, to be sent forward by mules as soon as possible; La Asunta having a good mule road, connecting it with La Paz.

20th.—A short distance above Charabamba, on the right bank, the mountain is perpendicular to the river, and has a beautiful cascade of 100 feet fall. Near by, the river is narrowed to 40 feet by two projecting points of rock, now six feet above the surface, making an almost impassable passage in high water. To-day we passed what on Colton's map is called Rio Vacas, but is in reality Arcopongo river.

21st.—We passed the river Tumanpaya, which comes from the valley of Chulumani. Our river has become quite small and rapid, being a steady pull for the men; the hills more open, and nearly free of trees, rising to 3000 or 4000 feet above us. Passing two very bad passes, we came, towards 3 P.M., to the Encañada de Veniqui. The valley is crossed by a solid rock more than a hundred feet high. Through this the river has cut a curved channel, leaving the walls perpendicular. Above, the river bed in high water is 500 feet wide. A sand-bar throws the river against the obstructing rock, which, turning its course, throws it directly against the side of the mountain, where it ascends to a height of 15 feet, crests and falls over, then rushes whirling into the narrow channel, and thus forming the most difficult and dangerous pass on the river. Here we nearly lost a balsa, and Mr. Fetterman his wife. We now meet maguey plants and the molle tree. The sides of the hills and sand-bars show traces of saltpetre. The mountains now have only grass on their summits instead of trees.

22nd.—We passed the river Zuri. Three miles above its mouth the river Vacas joins with the Zuri, forming the Zuri junction.

23rd.—We pulled our balsa out on dry land for the last time near the mouth of the river Miguillo, lat. 16° 29' 32" S. We now took mules and went west over the mountains into the Tumanpaya valley, and stopped at Irupana. Observations of a star in the south, another in the north, and a meridian altitude of the sun gave for Irupana 16° 29' 09" S. lat. At Miguillo we found 3360 feet elevation, having risen 1125 feet in a distance of 150 miles. Although we had been from May 15th till June 23rd in the ascent from Rurinabaque to Miguillo, it only takes seven or eight days to descend that distance.

July 21st.—We left Irupana with mules, and, returning to the river-bed, continued our ascent.

22nd.—We passed the Chungamayo, a stream coming from the snows of Illimani, whose snow-capped summit can be seen as we look up that ravine.

23rd.—We passed through the narrow gorges that the river has cut through, and passed the river Caricata, which was our extreme point south. We now direct our course to the north-west.

25th.—At 2.30 P.M. we arrived at La Paz, and thus brought to an end our ascent of the Beni and La Paz rivers. The Bolivian Government were much gratified with my work. La Paz has an elevation 11,985 feet.

Previous to the reading of Mr. Markham's paper,

The PRESIDENT said he need hardly remind the Meeting that Mr. Markham won his geographical spurs in Peru; for it was during his visit to Lima and Cuzco in 1853 that he laid the groundwork of his geographical reputation. He revisited the country in 1861, on a mission from the Government, in order to obtain living chinchona trees for transplanting in India. No doubt many present had read his account of that journey, and he (the President) could confidently recommend those to read it who had not as yet done so. Several papers had been read before the Society by Mr. Markham on this interesting country, one of which was on the distribution of the various primitive Peruvian tribes, and he had shown his continued interest in it by writing a history of that unfortunate war which had lately raged between Peru and Chili. The paper divided itself into two parts : one was a history of the exploration of the Amaru-mayu, the other the history of that of the Beni. Our knowledge of the Amaru-mayu was derived from notes of the travels of various Peruvian discoverers; the history of the Beni was derived chiefly from the recent journey of Dr. Heath, an American gentleman who had been employed as medical officer to those who were engaged in opening up the country under the direction of Colonel Church, who, he was happy to say, was present. Three years ago Mr. Minchin read a paper on Bolivia, a country which seemed to be endowed by nature with every element of future prosperity and greatness. The main feature, however, of the present paper was the account it gave of the sources in the Eastern Andes of the two great tributaries of the Amazons, which themselves were equal to the mightiest rivers of the continent of Europe. Colonel Church had been engaged in one of the greatest works connected with the future civilisation of South America that had ever been undertaken. They were aware that shipping of a very large size could ascend the Amazons and the Madeira until stopped by certain falls. Those falls alone prevented shipping finding its way to the very foot of the Eastern Andes, and it had been the labour of a considerable part of Colonel Church's life to discover means for overcoming that great natural obstacle.

After the paper,

Colonel G. E. CHURCH said that a year and a half ago, when crossing the Chimborazo Pass of the Andes, he met an old woman and her daughter, each with a large bundle of faggots on her back. As he jogged along on his mule he conversed with the woman about the condition of the common people in Ecuador. The finest locomotive machine of which she had any idea was a mule. Finally he gave her a two-real piece, about tenpence. She dropped her bundle of faggots, and looked at him from head to foot, and said, " What country are you from ? "   " From the United States." " How far is that from here ? "   " Well, that is about 1500 or 2000 leagues." She looked at him in wonderment, and said, " How young you must have been when you started ! " When he listened to Mr. Clements Markham's paper, ranging as it did over a vast space, and the marvellous accuracy of its detail, and the profound knowledge of geographical subjects, he felt like that old woman—" How young he must have been when he started ! " But Mr. Markham had been kind enough to leave a small part of the field without giving them the benefit of his knowledge of it, and he (Colonel Church) would say a few words with regard to it. The Andes, stretching along the west coast of South America, had their greatest counterfort towards the east, on the parallel of Cochabamba, and extending 123 leagues eastward from that city to the town of Santa Cruz de la Sierra, on one of the affluents of the Mamoré. On the western escarpment of the Andes the slope was not so steep as on the east. The clouds from the Atlantic Ocean became drier and drier until they reached the eastern base of the Andes, against which they beat, and produced very severe results. They rushed through great gorges, at the base of which there were great numbers of falls and rapids, until they reached the plain of the Beni. He believed that vast region was at one time a lake, bounded on the north-west by a range of hills which separated the Amaru-mayu from the Purus river, and having its north-eastern boundary on the Brazilian side. The northern and eastern side was Brazilian territory. On the south the lake must have met the great counterfort of the Andes, and been separated by it from the head-waters of the Paraguay river. The lake must have been held in place on the north by the falls of the river Madeira. One of his reasons for believing in this lake was that the upper course of the Purus river ran at a lower level than the Amaru-mayu ; and if there were not a line of hills separating it from the Purus, the Amaru-mayu would probably have found its way into the Purus, as a great many geographers believed it did. This vast lake must have had an area of about 200,000 square miles, but as the mountains were denuded it was filled with detritus, so that to-day there was an enormous plain, composed of fine sedimentary deposit, with scarcely a pebble for hundreds of miles; so much so, that the Indians in Exaltacion begged their friends, when they were going to the banks of the river Mamoré, to bring back a stone, so that they might see what a stone was like. Well, the lake was not entirely filled up, for even now about 40,000 square miles of the district were annually overflowed to a depth of from two to five feet for three months in the year. South of Trinidad, up to the base of the counterfort of the Andes, an enormous overflow takes place, leaving a sedimentary deposit of great fertility, just as in the case of the Nile. A very curious thing was noticeable there. There were a great many ant-hills in this district; they were little pyramids ranging from three to eight feet in height: during the flood season the ants retire to the top to get clear of the water. But how did the ants know that there was going to be a flood? All the inhabitants of the district would state that, when there was going to be an extraordinary flood, the ants went to work, and put an extra storey on the top of their house. The name of the Amaru-mayu was derived from the Quichua language; but he understood that the Takana tribes, five in number, who lived along the line of the Amaru-mayu, called it the Mayu-tata, or the "great father river." Mayu-tata was very similar to Manitou, in the North American tongue, and meant exactly the same thing. The word *tata* meaning "father," was also found in New Mexico and the Puebla language of North America, several thousand miles away from the Amaru-mayu. He might be allowed to diverge a little and remark that the tribes in New Mexico and the United States called the Apaches and Comanches, had the termination *che* which meant "people," while in southern South America there were the Tehuelche, Pehuenche, and Huelche tribes of Patagonia, having the termination *che* which meant the same thing. That was a very remarkable circumstance and was worthy of the study of ethnologists. He had personally sounded the Mamoré until it struck the falls of the Madeira. North and east of Cochabamba there were three large branches,—the Securé, the Chaparé, or middle river, and the Chimoré. The Securé was examined by D'Orbigny, the French naturalist, in 1845. D'Orbigny was the first discoverer of the *Victoria Regia*. The Chaparé was explored by Lieutenant Gibbon of the United States Navy, in 1854. He (Colonel Church) passed along the great counterfort of the Andes and descended the mountains to Santa Cruz de la Sierra. About ten leagues to the east of Cochabamba was the Rio Grande. That river was navigable, and he had it explored with a steam launch in 1873. They were able to ascend to within ten leagues of Santa Cruz de la Sierra. He himself explored the Mamoré. He commenced his soundings at the mouth of the Rio Grande in the dry season. The river was about 1200 feet wide and 10 feet deep. It was a gentle inclined plane to the first rapid of the Madeira, and gradually increased to a depth of 40 feet and a width of three-quarters of a mile. It was a noble stream running from two to three miles an hour and presenting every facility for splendid navigation. Coming into it from the eastward was the river Guaporé, the boundary-line between Brazil and Bolivia. There was a Portuguese fort there, built in the last century out of stone obtained at the falls of the Madeira, and taken up stream with great difficulty. At that time, owing to the wars of the Spaniards, the Portuguese, in order to communicate with their Matto Grosso possessions, annually sent fleets of canoes carrying about four tons each. These canoes were dragged round the falls. In 1882 he (Colonel Church) descended the La Paz river from the south of La Paz to about 130 miles, and then embarked on rafts to go down to Reyes. Along the La Paz river, nature was at work as in prehistoric times. La Paz was situated in a gorge 1000 feet below the plain of Titicaca. As the city was approached nothing but the roofs of houses was seen. One thousand feet represented the visible thickness of a vast mass of drift matter, and as the river was descended, lateral streams were met with which were caused by the

terrific storms which sometimes raged in the Andes. These storms were local.
They swept down vast masses of detritus, and dammed up the main river, which
rose against the dam, overflowed it, and swept the detritus again across the stream
from which it received it.   He had seen those beds of detritus at least 400 feet thick
with gigantic boulders weighing many tons, and the stiff clay of the formation
cemented the boulders together almost perpendicularly.   A story was told of one of
the Incas of Peru, in the mythology of the Indians, which he thought rivalled anything ever done by Zeus.   It was said that one of the Incas having had a quarrel
(it was not said with whom—perhaps it was his wife), got very vexed, and sweeping
his hand round with a royal gesture struck the top of Mount Churuguella, about
18,000 feet high.   He knocked the top off to the south-west, and there it stood to
the present day, the beautiful cone of Sajama, snow-capped, 19,000 feet high.   In
crossing from the La Paz river over to Chayanta, across the mountains, he discovered
that the mule traffic in the range had worn out the road to a depth of six or eight
feet.   There was a terrace there covered with about five feet of vegetable earth, and
gigantic forests on the top of it.   All that country had been densely populated in
very remote times, and was sometimes terraced right up to the snow-line, showing
how precious the ground was and the labour that was expended upon it to make it
useful.   The depth of the terrace below the surface, and the forest trees above it,
showed that the population must have resided there many centuries ago.   The
inhabitants of the country which was the subject of consideration that evening
numbered perhaps from two and a half to three millions, mostly living on the higher
lands and just over the eastern slope of the Andes.   The city of La Paz, for instance,
had 80,000 inhabitants, and Cochabamba 60,000.   They were a very peculiar people.
At each post-house where he stopped he noticed blood on the walls of every
bedroom, and blood at the entrance, and it was a long time before he could discover
what it meant.   At last he was told that it was the custom every year to let
the post-houses to different persons, who immediately whitewashed them and
then killed a goat or a sheep and sprinkled the blood over the walls with the
object of bringing luck to the post-house during the year, and "giving the
walls something to eat."   There was another curious custom.   Riding along
the roads among the Andes the traveller found little piles of stones ranging
from six inches to one foot high, apparently placed on one another with the
greatest care.   It was very difficult to ascertain why that was done; but he discovered that, when an Indian started off on a journey with his mules or llamas
or jackasses, and expected to be absent five or six days, he wished to know whether
everything was going on all right at home, and so he formed these little piles of
stones.   The more jealous he was, the more delicate he made the piles, and if when
he returned home the pile of stones had fallen down, then good-bye to all domestic
felicity.   In former times Jesuits occupied all the country up to the Madeira,
and even towards the Madre de Dios.   They crossed the Gran Chaco, and formed
thirteen different settlements along the Mamoré, the San Miguel, the Magdalena,
and other tributaries, and succeeded in doing great and good work.   The action of
the Spanish Government in 1767 in driving the Jesuits out of the country had almost
blotted those settlements from the face of the earth.   In 1871 he ascended the mouth
of the Beni for a few miles, but did not go up to the first fall.   It was a grand river,
and in the rainy season he should think it carried more water than the Mississippi.
In ascending the Madeira, five falls were met with above the mouth of the Beni,
and fourteen falls or rapids below it.   Among the worst of the falls was the Cauldron
of Hell; that was the rapid where Colonel Maldonado was wrecked, and he (Colonel
Church) was very nearly wrecked there.   It was customary in passing those falls to
drag the canoes over the rocks.   After about two or three days of terrible work

they got to the lower end of the falls, a distance of about two miles. As the traveller approached the fall he saw a vast wall of foam nearly crossing the river, and in the midst of the rapid on the right was an immense whirlpool, and on the left another. The river swelled up in the middle for about the width of 40 or 50 feet. He had had a little experience of his Indian crew at the mouth of the Beni, where he had gone over a fall, and stove his canoe to pieces, and had to use threats to keep his Indians in the canoe. He expected, like other travellers, to haul the canoe overland at the Cauldron of Hell; but he got caught in a current, and found himself being hurled against the wall of foam. But just before reaching it an eddy took the canoe and carried it towards the eastern shore, around the wall of foam, and confronting the whirlpools. He showed his revolver, and compelled the captain of the canoe to steer as he was directed. His crew consisted of twelve Indians, speaking five different tongues, and not understanding each other. They reached the lower end of the Cauldron of Hell in two minutes, as near as he could judge, instead of two days, and they did not upset either. Just below the Cauldron of Hell they saw forty or fifty savages standing on the bank of the Madeira. Those savages were always very good-natured if one knew how to treat them; but if the traveller did not know how to treat them, he was very apt to get scalped or murdered. He caused his canoe to be steered straight for the bank. The savages sent the women and children into the bushes, got their bows and arrows ready, and had them bent. He held out his hand towards them, jumped ashore, and walked up the bank. They lowered their bows and arrows, shook hands with him, and he gave them some fish-hooks, with which they were immensely pleased. In return they gave him large bunches of bananas. He invited the chief and four or five of his men to go off to an island and dine with him. It was the strangest dinner-party he ever gave. Those fellows were clothed in what Mark Twain would call "smiles." The young chief was about thirty years of age; his hair was cut across his forehead, and hung loosely down his shoulders; two capivara teeth, about as long as a man's finger, were passed through his ears, and were held in place by a string which came under his chin. Around each wrist was a band of black palm leaf, and round each ankle, which set off the contour of his finely developed limbs. His eyes were everywhere, and he seemed to see everything. In the United States, when a person admired a man, the first thing he did was to say, "Will you take a drink?" That was the first thing he said to the chief. He had some rum which he had purchased at Santa Cruz de la Sierra, which had not been diluted. He poured out a glassful, and handed it to the savage. The chief handed it back to him, and intimated that he ought to taste it first. He did so, and the chief then put it to his mouth, and at the same time put his left hand to his throat, and as the liquor poured down his throat, burning all the way, he said, "Ugh, ugh, ugh." Then he struck himself on the breast, and said "Yocaré!" meaning his tribe. He knew two or three words of Portuguese, and said, "Capitão," and very unexpectedly he drew off like a prize-fighter, and struck him (Colonel Church) in the chest, and said, "Grand capitão." They had a very charming dinner-party.

The Incas certainly carried their conquests to the Beni river, south of Cavinas. A road about 25 feet wide could be traced for some distance towards Cuzco from there and he had traced the Inca occupation to the slope leading down to Santa Cruz de la Sierra, and into the Argentine Republic, 400 miles south of the Bolivian frontier. The picture-writing around the Madeira falls was very strange, and he had seen very similar writing in New Mexico, made by the Apache Indians or their predecessors. The rainfall in this district was from 84 to 90 inches per annum, and that might be said to be the average rainfall on the southern side of the Amazon river. On the northern side it was heavier, at Panama being 126 inches. The health of the country was as good as that of any semi-tropical or tropical country. Of the twenty-eight engineers sent out in one party, and remaining eighteen months at the fall of San Antonio, twenty-seven returned in perfectly good health. He supposed that the object of the Geographical Society was to be the pioneers of progress and civilisation, and to lead the way to enterprise ; he might therefore be pardoned if he said something about the work which was projected around the falls of the Madeira to open up a district which was twice the size of France. The work was originally organised under concessions from the Governments of Bolivia and Brazil. The money was raised and put in trust for it, and the whole thing was going bravely on, with 1200 men at work, a locomotive running over the first five miles of line, 40 or 50 miles of material on the ground, and ocean steamers running right up to the rapids of the Madeira, 1600 miles from the sea, when opposition succeeded in wrecking the enterprise, and dividing the money among the subscribers. That was in consequence of the revocation of the concessions made by Bolivia. An agent was sent to Bolivia, with instructions to obtain the revocation, and his success was only too great. But the enterprise was not dead. The rivers along which the whole commerce would pass pointed straight for London and Liverpool. To reach that beautiful valley by any other route would cost from 50l. to 60l. per ton for all the goods taken there; but when once the falls of the Madeira were avoided, as rich a field for trade and emigration would be opened up as could be found anywhere in South America. Recently he was in Brazil, where he was received most kindly by his Imperial Majesty, Don Pedro, whose grand qualities as a man and monarch needed no eulogy from him, and the Emperor told him he considered that enterprise to be first in importance in his empire. The largest and best corps of engineers ever organised in the country had recently been sent to the falls of the Madeira, not only to re-examine the whole of the projected line of railway, but to ascend the river, and make a railway survey from the head of navigation to the capital of the great province of Matto Grosso. On their return new concessions would be given to reorganise the enterprise, and they would be given under the guarantee of the capital by Brazil, which would insure the raising of the necessary funds. That would open up the whole of Southern Peru, two-thirds of Bolivia, and the whole western part of Brazil. All that was required was the extension of the railway from Cuzco down to the Piñi-Piñi, or to the head of the navigation of the Amaru-mayu, to open up an interoceanic route which for beauty of scenery and interest to the tourist had few equals on the face of the globe.

Mr. CHRISTY asked Mr. Markham if he could tell what variety of the indiarubber tree it was from which the indiarubber was obtained.

Mr. CLEMENTS MARKHAM replied that it was pretty clearly established that the trees on the western slopes of the Andes, where the forests reached the Pacific Ocean, belonged to the genus *Castilloa*, and that all within the Amazons basin on the eastern slopes were the genus *Hevea*.

Mr. CHRISTY said that both those indiarubbers were of the greatest importance to commerce. There were now many branches of trade really languishing for want of reliable sources of indiarubber. Many indiarubbers were brought to this country, but it was found that they were collected from young trees, and did not harden properly; but the rubbers coming from Brazil were of extreme importance. He could corroborate the remark as to the large quantities of gold found in the country. He had lately had stopping with him a gentleman who had resided near La Paz, and who told him that great profits were obtained there by dealers in the gold collected in the district.

Sir HARRY VERNEY said he was extremely glad to hear from Mr. Markham that his old friend General Miller had done something for the increase of geographical knowledge. He knew him in his ministerial capacity and as an administrator both in Cuzco and on the Pacific coast, but he was not aware, until he heard it from Mr. Markham, that he had done anything towards the extension of geographical knowledge. He was one of those " Englishmen abroad" who did much to ennoble the character of the English nation in South America. No one contributed more greatly than General Miller to the freedom of the South American countries from the Spanish rule and to improve the character of the population. He recollected Sir Woodbine Parish at Buenos Ayres telling him what was corroborated by Colonel Church—that the Incas had descended the rivers and had come down the La Plata ; that they had met Indians from the Amazons, and that they had fought in the vicinity of the two rivers. Mr. Clements Markham had referred to the different navigators of the Amazons, but he did not mention that our own countryman Lieutenant Lister Maw in 1828 or 1829 obtained permission to leave his ship at Callao, and came down the Amazons. He told him (Sir Harry Verney) that 4000 miles from the mouth of the Amazons there was an enormous basin where two large rivers met, and that the basin was large enough to hold the whole British fleet. He rejoiced to hear what Colonel Church had told them with regard to the probability of commercial enterprise penetrating into those interesting and most remarkable districts ; and in the high character of the present Emperor of Brazil they had a guarantee that every opportunity would be given for the extension of commerce and civilisation in that productive region.

The PRESIDENT said it was sixty years ago that Sir Harry Verney rode from the eastern coast of America across the Andes to the western shore. He wished to ask Colonel Church what became of the inhabitants of the vast level plain which he had spoken of during the three or four months when it was flooded.

Colonel CHURCH answered that there were no inhabitants in the greater portion of it. At Exaltacion, an old Jesuit mission, there were 3000 inhabitants, and the streets of the town were only one foot out of water in the wet season, and 20 or 25 feet in the dry season. All over the district there were little rises in the land generally occupied by all kinds of waterfowl and animals that sought shelter there while the intermediate parts were flooded. The line of the Mamoré river had a fringe of trees. The animals were very numerous. The greater portion of the population of Bolivia were on the slopes of the Andes, but nothing produced in the Mocos valley had been of any use except for home consumption, on account of the difficulty of transport over the passes of the Andes 14,800 feet high.

The PRESIDENT said that in listening to the description given in Mr. Markham's interesting paper, and to Colonel Church's original observations, he was struck by the recollection of Buckle's remarks about the country, in which he insisted upon the effect of natural causes upon the development of the human race. In speaking of South America he said that was a case where the prodigious proportions of nature actually overpowered and crushed the efforts of man : the forests were so vast, the streams so broad and rapid, the mountains so huge, that nature was too much for him to contend with ; and certainly when it was considered that the country had been for 300 years in the possession of a race so valiant and enterprising as the Spanish were in olden days, of the continuance of which qualities there was ample proof in the story of Peruvian explorations on the Amaru-mayu, it would seem as if the explanation given by Buckle was the only one which could account for the obscurity of a land which in many respects had so much to attract enterprise. At the same time, if there were many Colonel Churches and Dr. Heaths in the world it would not be long before a great deal more was known of Bolivia, and Buckle's philosophical views negatived by the results of experience.

2 A 2

Departure of the Dutch Arctic Expedition, 1883.

THE sixth voyage of the *Willem Barents* to the Arctic Seas is specially important, because its principal object is to bring succour to the Danish exploring vessel *Dijmphna*, and to the steamer *Varna*, which were beset in the Kara Sea, and of which nothing has been heard since last September.

The Dutch Arctic Committee have shown most praiseworthy continuity of purpose in organising the annual voyages. Their first conception, and the enthusiasm which led to the subscription of sufficient funds in 1878, were due to the energy and persuasive eloquence of young Koolemans Beynen, whose melancholy death was so deeply regretted by all geographers. His was a noble character, and he was inspired with the true spirit of Arctic research. Our accomplished honorary associate, Commodore Jansen, who was very warmly attached to young Beynen, has since promoted the continuance of the work, and has brought his varied experience and great nautical knowledge to the counsels of the Dutch Arctic Committee, which is composed as follows :—Fransen van de Putte (*President*); Commodore Jansen (*Vice-President*); Baron Wassenaer van Catwyck; Captain de Bruyne, Captain Bruekhuysen (former commanders of the *Willem Barents*); Charles Boissevain; Mr. Schorer (*Royal Commissioner of North Holland*); E. N. Rahusen.

During the first voyage, in 1878, when De Bruyne commanded the *Willem Barents*, and Koolemans Beynen was his second, a very complete reconnaissance was made of the Spitzbergen and Barents Seas. In 1879, when De Bruyne was again in command, Franz-Josef Land was for the first time sighted in open water. The voyages of 1880 and 1881 were commanded by Captain Bruekhuysen, that of 1882 by Captain Hoffman. When Mr. Leigh Smith retreated from Franz-Josef Land in his boats, the *Willem Barents* was the first vessel he sighted; and when the *Hope* got on shore, Sir Allen Young received effective assistance from the *Willem Barents*, whose carpenter, Mr. Latjes, worked hard at the needful repairs. Every year the Dutch explorers, by their numerous observations, their soundings and dredgings, and their other work, have contributed usefully to the advancement of geographical science. At the same time a number of officers and men have been trained to ice navigation. The naval officers are only allowed to serve for two years continuously, so that there is a regular succession of them acquiring Arctic experience. When an officer has served two years the Arctic Committee presents him with a handsome piece of plate, about eighteen inches high, called the "Barents Cup." The figure of Barents holding the Dutch flag stands on a globe, forming the cover and bowl, which is engraved with the old chart of Barents. The whole is supported on silver dolphins. The men who have served two years receive silver tobacco-boxes of antique pattern.

For the voyage of 1883 the *Willem Barents* was carefully overhauled, and found to be thoroughly seaworthy and as sound as ever: as well adapted to encounter the ice as any sailing vessel that ever entered it. Her commander is Lieutenant Dalen, who was first-lieutenant in the last voyage, a steady and efficient officer. Under him are three young lieutenants, who go out full of enthusiasm for the cause of geographical discovery. Lieutenants J. and M. Kluit are twin brothers, and the other is Lieutenant Phaff. The surgeon and naturalist is Dr. Waelchli, and Mr. Grant accompanies his Dutch friends as photographer, for the fourth time. Our indefatigable Associate has now made seven voyages to the Arctic regions, of which four were on board the *Willem Barents*. Latjes, the carpenter, has been every voyage, and of the crew of seven men and a boy, three belong to the Navy. One lad is sent out by the old town of Enckhuysen with a view to promoting enterprise among the fishermen of the Zuyder Zee, and he is to receive a prize of 100 gulden if his commander reports well of him.

It will be remembered that last year a party was sent out, under the auspices of Professor Buys Ballot, of Utrecht, to form a Dutch meteorological station at Port Dickson, near the mouth of the Yenisei. The expedition was accompanied by Lieutenant Lamie, of the Dutch Navy, who had formerly served in the *Willem Barents*, but the steamer *Varna*, which took out the observers and their stores and apparatus, was commanded by a German. The steamer *Luisa*, under Captain Burmeister, was also chartered to take out some of the materials for the observatory. The *Luisa* appears to have parted company near the Kara Strait, and reported that the *Varna* and the Danish exploring vessel *Dijmphna*, commanded by Lieutenant Hovgaard, were beset in the ice near the middle of the Kara Sea, and in sight of each other. They were last seen by the *Luisa* on September 26th, 1882. Much anxiety is felt for the safety of the *Varna*, as she was not fortified for ice navigation, and was very deep in the water.

The possibility of succouring these vessels has received much attention from the Arctic Committee. The instructions to Lieutenant Dalen are that the *Willem Barents* is to proceed to Vardoe, and then to make the best of her way to Waigatz, and attempt to enter the Kara Sea by the southern strait. If the strait is closed she is to go to Archangel to see whether there is any news of the missing ships, and to communicate with the Committee. She is then to return to the Kara Strait, and to search the east coast of Waigatz and Novaya Zemlya for boats or men. If nothing is found, and there is no news, she is to attempt to reach Port Dickson. In the event of favourable tidings, and of news being received that the *Dijmphna* and *Varna* are safe, an examination of the Kara Sea is to be undertaken, and collections are to be made there, as in the Barents Sea during former voyages.

The *Willem Barents* was ready for sea, and was to sail on Saturday, the 5th of May. In the previous evening the Arctic Committee gave a farewell dinner to the officers. Commodore Jansen presided, and Mr. Leigh Smith and Mr. Clements Markham (Secretary R. G. S.) were among the guests. Mr. Leigh Smith described his feelings of relief and joy when he first sighted the *Willem Barents* at the end of his long and perilous retreat from Franz-Josef Land, and, in memory of the event, he presented the mess of the Dutch Arctic vessel with two silver cups. Mr. Markham, in the name of the President and Council of the Royal Geographical Society, expressed warm sympathy and admiration for the perseverance and energy of the Dutch Committee, and for the skill and gallantry of the officers and crew of the *Willem Barents*. Next morning the little vessel left Amsterdam, and proceeded down the canal amidst great enthusiasm. The burgomaster stood on the quay, surrounded by a crowd of people whose hearty cheers mingled with the strains of a military band. Several members of the Committee, Mr. Leigh Smith and Mr. Clements Markham, continued on board the *Willem Barents* as far as Ij-muyden, where Sir Allen Young, who had been detained, also came on board. Two racing-boats, manned by young students of Utrecht and Leyden, pulled all the way, one on each side, and every vessel in the canal kept up the cheering with hearty goodwill. At Ij-muyden the guests were transferred on board a steamer commanded by Captain de Bruyne, the first commander of the *Willem Barents*. The two vessels went out of harbour together, and, after proceeding with the exploring vessel for a short distance, the steamer parted company with three ringing cheers. The sea was smooth, and the *Willem Barents* made sail to a fresh breeze. She commenced her adventurous voyage, in which the cause of humanity is linked with that of science, under the happiest auspices.

GEOGRAPHICAL NOTES.

Progress in North Borneo.—The diary of Mr. L. B. von Donop from July 30th, 1882, to January 17th last, recently published in the *Ceylon Observer*, contains many details of interest as to the topography and products of the central and western parts of the new North Borneo territory of Sabah, though this observer's explorations were confined to the region already broadly sketched by the late Captain Witti. His first journey was from Kudat in Marudu Bay, in the extreme north of the territory, to Abai on the west coast, from which an excursion was made to the country watered by the Jampassuk. This consists of undulating hills covered in many instances with fodder-grass as high as a man's head; the soil appeared very rich, coffee and paddy being grown, and a growth of fine timber-trees round the chief's house presented the appearance of an English park. From this point Mr. von Donop struck south towards Kinabalu, passing through a very hilly but cultivated country to Tambutuan and Kian. A projected journey to Kinabalu from the latter place had to be abandoned, but the ascent of a neighbouring ridge 4700 feet high afforded a good view of the intervening thickly-wooded ranges and valleys. Arrived at Tuan, range after range was seen, mostly with jungle on the top ridges but cultivated beneath, and after crossing the Yaggo river the rich and promising Danoe plain was reached, different aspects of Kinabalu being observed as the route worked gradually round it. Mr. von Donop finally reached the Kinarum river after passing various villages and finding a succession of ranges and well-watered valleys, and he then struck north to Bongon, returning to Kudat by boat. In September he again proceeded to Kinarum to join the late Mr. Frank Hatton, and after excursions to Bongon and various points on the Marudu river, once more made for Kian, spending some days in the Sissio country, on the northern side of Kinabalu. This, with the Tambuyukan ranges on the east, was found to comprise many thousand acres, varying in elevation from 700 feet to 4000 feet, and of a very promising nature. A partial ascent of Tambuyukan was made, and the land found available for cocoa, pepper, and Liberian coffee on the lower elevations, and tea, chinchona, &c., on the higher. In the beginning of October, Mr. von Donop started from Kinarum eastward for the Sugut country, returning to Kudat northwards by the Benkoka. From his account and other notices of North Borneo, it appears that a considerable part of the available land in Sandakan Bay has already been taken up for agricultural purposes, Mr. E. Major's company having taken 50,000 acres, Mr. A. Major 40,000 acres, Mr. de Lissa 20,000 acres, Mr. Lo Yuen-Yno's Shanghai company 10,000 acres, Messrs. Wilson and Smith, tobacco-planters from Deli, 10,000 acres, &c. Buildings also are being rapidly raised, the families of settlers who have arrived seeming to find the climate healthy; and the rate of progress may be estimated from the fact that an official newspaper was started in April under the name of *The North Borneo Herald.*

The Republic of Ecuador.—In June 1881, Colonel G. E. Church, then at Quito, received instructions from the United States Government to supply a report on the geography, commerce, and general condition of Ecuador, which he submitted in the following September, his information being derived almost entirely from original sources and personal observation. This Report, for a copy of which we are indebted to him, forms Executive Document No. 69, 47th Congress, 2nd Session, ordered to be printed February 27th last; and is important as a recent account of the Republic by a competent and keen observer. In discussing its geographical limits, Colonel Church points out that all the boundary lines are untraced, except that defined by the Pacific, so that the exact area of the country is unknown, though it may be estimated at about 150,000 geographical square miles; the quoted ancient limits, all that exist in fact, are deficient in mathematical data, and leave " as fertile a field for discussion as any Spanish-American could wish." The area, as estimated by Colonel Church, will be observed to differ materially from that given by Behm and Wagner, which is 643,295 square kilometres, or 187,800 geographical square miles (248,380 statute square miles).

Colonel Church, in sketching broadly the geography and topography of Ecuador, divides it into three great sections by the double line of the Andes, composed of the Pacific coast and the inland ranges, which run nearly parallel from 40 to 60 miles apart. The latter throws out numerous immense and long spurs on its eastern face, between which rise great affluents of the Amazons, whilst the former possesses only short and precipitous spurs, contributing to the river systems of Western Ecuador. Between the two ranges lies a plateau, 7000 feet high on the Colombian border, rising gradually to 9500 feet at Quito, and more or less maintaining that elevation to the Peruvian frontier, where it descends to 7000 feet. On this plateau are short and broken ridges, sometimes almost connecting the two ranges from east to west, and cutting it into eight subdivisions, themselves more or less scored by cañons, small rivers, &c., and possessing but a small area of stunted forest lands. Enumerating the mighty peaks of both ranges, of which ten are still more or less volcanic, Colonel Church remarks that, as one rides through the river gorges, geological sections are exposed, hundreds of feet in thickness, of volcanic rock and ash alternating with thin caps of earth, showing what a perfect furnace of nature Ecuador must have been. The erupted ash has, however, fertilising qualities, and is soon covered with vegetation, resulting in a productive layer of humus. Very different from this comparatively unproductive and arid inter-Andean section, are those both to its east and west. The former, or Amazons section, is completely forest-covered; the dry winds which leave the African coast and become thoroughly saturated during their transit of the Atlantic, reach their acme of precipitation as they approach the numerous snowy peaks of Ecuador, and give birth to a dense and rank growth of vegetation on the eastern foot-hills of the Andes. On the west, also, which receives the rain-clouds of the Pacific, most of the lands are forest-covered, the trees becoming larger and taller the nearer the base of the ridge of the Andes is approached, until in the gorges of the western spurs the very hot-houses of nature are found, steaming under a tropical sun, and forcing into existence a prodigal vegetation, where each plant has to wage war for existence against its fellows. This Pacific section must have been at no very remote geological period an archipelago, the islands of which were the outposts of the Andes, presenting hills and slaty ridges rising from 50 to 3000 feet above the ocean, and having a certain parallelism with the Andean chain. The slow uplifting of the coast-line and the denudation of the cordillera have filled up the intervals between these former islands to such an elevation that the floods of the rainy season do not cover the low lands except in the Guayaquil valley, where also the filling - up process threatens rapidly to destroy the utility of Guayaquil itself as a port.

A rapid review of the river system shows that at least 2500 miles are suitable for steamboat navigation on the Amazons side, and probably as much more for boats; whilst on the western side there are some 500 miles.

As to climate, the rainy season is usually from December to June, the remaining months being called dry; on the Amazons slope it rains all the year round. As regards the influence of climate on man, there are vast healthy districts in the river valleys of the Amazons region, whilst those of the Pacific shore are commonly full of disease. Any special disorders appear to be chiefly due there to the lack of sanitary measures, and in the west and north-western parts to the abuse of sweets as food, which results in a curious and frightful intestinal complaint.

The country is, and must apparently remain, almost wholly agricultural, the Pacific coast and river valleys of both east and west yielding generous crops of cacao, sugar-cane, cotton, rice, coffee, tobacco, and tropical fruits, whilst the inter-Andean plateau produces all the cereals and vegetables incident to a temperate and even cold climate (though of inferior quality), and in favoured localities sugar-cane and maize. No hope of its ever being an exporter of cereals is held out; and cattle do not thrive in the Amazons section—chiefly, it is believed, from the immense number of bats which bleed or otherwise irritate them. Chinchona bark, for which the world was first indebted to the province of Loja, is now being so rapidly cut and sent out of the country without any attempt at planting for the future, that the supply must soon cease; and Colonel Church does not hesitate to record the opinion that the highest official sanction is given to this destructive measure for private emolument. In mineral wealth, Ecuador is probably one of the poorest of the South American States, containing on the western slopes only a few (and not rich) alluvial deposits of gold, which are more abundant in the valleys of the Amazons section. The provinces of Azuay and Loja are the only ones giving indications of valuable mines warranting the investment of capital.

The population is estimated as 1,000,000 at the most, exclusive of savage tribes, divided as follows: White, 100,000; mixed, 300,000; pure Indian, 600,000. (Behm and Wagner give 946,033 from official returns in 1878.) The pure Indians are Quichua, more genial in expression than those of Bolivia and Peru, but with no apparent elements for the re-creation of a manly nation. Their language is not so pure as the Bolivian Quichua, being split into several dialects more or less mixed with Spanish. The evil qualities of the mixed races are briefly condemned as the source of the degradation of the country.

After lucidly discussing the internal administration of the Republic, Colonel Church points out the importance of the Putumayo and Caqueta affluents of the Amazons as trade routes, and enters at some length upon the possibilities of creating internal communications, of which scarcely any now exist. Personally interested in the construction of future railroads, he is nevertheless of opinion that a thorough system of first-class mule routes would be the best for Ecuador for the next ten or twenty years.

The Report contains a short notice of the Galápagos Islands, which were annexed in 1832, and colonised through the energy of General Villamil, who was subsequently thwarted in every way by his Government. The islands are now practically abandoned, and have relapsed into their old condition, save for the increase of Villamil's cattle. The occupation by Ecuador is considered not to exist to a sufficient extent to entitle it to the respect of other nations.

In spite of the numerous and great natural advantages of the Republic, Colonel Church is compelled to admit that his report is not favourable ; and he summarises his reasons in the sentence :—" Until the patriotic element unites to strengthen municipal power, finances, and privileges, Ecuador will have neither prosperity and republicanism at home, nor honour abroad."

Obituary.

James Young, of Kelly.—The death of this much-respected member of the Society is recorded as having occurred on the 13th of May at his residence, Kelly, on the Firth of Clyde, in the seventy-first year of his age. He was widely known for his discoveries in practical chemistry, particularly with regard to the extraction of a light-oil, or paraffin, from coal products, for illuminating purposes, and for the new industry he thereupon founded in the neighbourhood of Glasgow. In the annals of geography his name will always occupy an honoured place through its connection with that of Dr. Livingstone, whose schemes of exploration and philanthropy he supported with his steady sympathy and pecuniary aid. When, in 1871, after two and a half years had elapsed without direct tidings of Livingstone, then wandering in the remote interior, our Society decided on organising an expedition for his search and relief, and the funds collected were sufficient only for one such expedition from the eastern side of Africa, he made an offer through his friend the Rev. Horace Waller to our President, Sir Henry Rawlinson, to equip at his own sole cost, a similar expedition from the west coast, it being thought probable that Livingstone on finding that the Lualaba was not, as he had supposed, connected with the Nile, but trended towards the Congo, would try to find his way to the Atlantic along the course of that river. The expedition was intrusted to the command of Lieutenant Grandy, R.N., who after failing, as others have done since, to force his way by the land route from San Salvador, and hitting at last on the only practicable entry into the interior along the banks of the Congo, was recalled on news of Livingstone's death reaching England. The expenses of the expedition amounted to 3041*l.* But he was a generous benefactor also in his own special domain of chemistry. He endowed Anderson's College, where he received his first instruction in chemistry by attending as a youth the lectures of Professor Graham, with a chair of practical chemistry, and presented his native city of Glasgow with a bronze statue of his teacher, for whose memory he entertained a lasting regard.

CORRESPONDENCE.

An Excursion in the Interior of New Guinea.

PORT MORESBY, NEW GUINEA, *February 7th*, 1883.

DEAR SIR,—We have recently returned from an interesting journey into the interior and visit to the Rouna falls. This is not quite new ground, but the falls have been only visited by a few, and I do not think any account of them has been published. The journey was new in one respect: Mrs. Lawes made one of the party, and was thus the first white lady to tread the "unbeaten tracks" of New Guinea.

Our object was twofold : first, to see the Rouna falls, and secondly, to visit the district of Taburo and Sogere at the back of the Astrolabe Mountains. Our party consisted of Mrs. Lawes, Mr. Chalmers, and self, with about twenty natives as carriers, &c.

Our first day's journey was on horse to the village of Rabadomu, about 15 miles from here in an easterly direction. We slept there, and started on foot at daybreak next morning. The mountain we had to ascend was right before us, covered with a light mantle of cloud. But before we reached its base we had to ascend and descend many times—sometimes as high as 300 feet and then down again to sea-level. The sun was high by the time we reached a pretty little creek at the foot of the mountain proper. We rested here a while and then prepared for the ascent. Mrs. Lawes had as guide and companion a trusty Koitapu native, who was very proud of his office.

We had three aneroids with us, one of the R. G. S. and two smaller of Steward's. The mean of readings at base of mountain was 608. The first part of the ascent was by a narrow but shady path, and this brought us to within 700 feet of the top. The last piece was a sheer ascent up the perpendicular face of the mountain. From below it seemed impossible that any path could be made up it, but we found a narrow zigzag track which brought us by a step at a time to the top. Mrs. Lawes was among the first at the summit. The mean of our aneroids gave 2600 feet, so that the actual height would be 1992 feet. The boiling-point thermometer read 211·6° at the bottom, and 207·6° at the top, with temperature at 80°, which would make the height of mountain 2320 feet.

The native name of the mountain is Veriata. We had a grand view from the top. As far as the eye could see was a panorama of sea and coast, hill and valley, intersected by many winding rivers and streams. At our feet ran the Laloke, and at our right hand could be plainly heard the roar of Rouna, although hidden from our view.

Our track lay in an easterly direction for about four miles, when we reached one of the Taburo villages, where, until quite recently, we had a mission teacher. His house was in good preservation, and we made it our headquarters while inland.

On the following day we visited the falls. They are not far from the teacher's house. An hour brought us quite to them at a leisurely pace. Long before that the river opened up. This valley of the Laloke forms one of the finest views I have seen in New Guinea. On this, the eastern side, the ground slopes away to the river, covered with rugged boulders and stunted vegetation. On the western side the cliffs rise almost perpendicularly to a height of 300 feet in the highest part, the summit and every crack or crevice being covered with vegetation. At the feet of these the river winds over a rocky, uneven bed, strewn with huge boulders forming a series of cascades. Standing as we did on the way down, looking up the valley northward, we could see the course of the river for two or three miles. It takes a sudden bend at the falls, so that you do not see the river above and below them from the same place.

You see nothing of the falls until you are just over them, and then to look down is enough to make any but a native dizzy. The stream is broken just above the fall by a huge boulder lying at an angle of about 45°, and about 60 feet in length on the upper face. Between this and the falls is a small rocky island covered with creeping palms and tropical vegetation. Just at the break were several bare rocks in mid-stream, on which some of our native boys stood with folded arms looking down into the abyss below.

The river was low, but in the rainy season all these rocks, now bare, are covered. The principal fall is on the eastern side, the greatest body of water falls over here, but about 100 feet lower down it breaks on a flat perpendicular rock. On the western side there was less water, but it is a sheer fall right to the bottom, where there is a terrible cauldron. We had no difficulty in getting right down to the stream, and standing in the shallow water at the side looking over the fall itself. There is a small friendly tree there which one can hold on to for safety. Here we read the aneroids and boiled a spirit-lamp for boiling-point. The former gave respectively 1150 and 1350, and the boiling-point thermometer 209·8°.

We inquired of the natives if there was any road to the bottom; they said it was possible but very difficult. But the offer of a tomahawk induced one to act as guide, and Mr. Chalmers went with him. They reached the bottom and made their way to the base of the falls. Here the aneroids registered 900 and 1100. This makes the height of fall exactly 250 feet by both aneroids. The boiling-point thermometer read 210·4°. The temperature was 80°; with the correction for this I make the difference between top and bottom 347 feet. We were very careful in marking the exact boiling-point. I suppose the river at the head of the falls to be about 50 yards wide, and below it is a series of small waterfalls, descending very rapidly. In the wet season there must be an enormous rush of water down this narrow bed. We saw from the debris at the top of some of the rocks how high it sometimes rises.

After a few days' rest at Tabure we went on to the district of Sogere, about 18 or 20 miles in an east by northerly direction. Our track was over a level country, and certainly well watered. We had to cross the Laloke an hour after starting. It is often unfordable here, but we were fortunate in finding it low. The current was very strong, and the bed of the river very uneven, but two or three joining hands, we got across without any mishap.

Soon after crossing the river we came to the solitary house of one of the Sogere chiefs. He installed himself as our guide and spokesman, and was very useful, although he had a great weakness for making speeches on every and no occasion. Our road lay through forest country, and for mile after mile we met no one and saw no house or garden. The trees were grand, especially some pandanus and banyans; beautiful mosses were on the damp ground, with a network of creepers and an occasional orchid overhead, while the wild strawberries and raspberries reminded us of our distant home.

Birds of paradise (*Paradisea raggiana*) were to be heard all the time, and now and then the clear note of the bell bird rung through the woods, so like a bell as to puzzle even familiar ears. The spell, however, of all this was often rudely broken by a muddy river or stream to cross. This was generally done by a New Guinea bridge, viz. a fallen tree. The round, smooth, slippery trunk was good enough bridge for the natives with their bare feet, but awkward enough for us in boots. It did not make one feel any steadier to know that crocodiles were plentiful in many of these streams. We were bitten, however, by nothing worse than leeches, and these caused no end of amusement. The weeds and grass by the roadside in damp places swarmed with them, and they fastened on to any bare legs they could touch.

The district of Sogere, like all the other inland ones we know, consists of small scattered villages, rarely more than eight or ten houses in a village, and often only three or four. The village at which we camped consisted of seven houses, and three tree houses, which are really forts or castles. One was 120 feet high. One of the natives went up with an armful of spears and threw them down at an imaginary enemy. When they have reason to expect an enemy they take up a supply of big stones. These houses command the whole village, and from their height could not easily be taken.

On our return we found every small ditch swollen into a muddy river, and when we got to the Laloke it had risen so much as to be unfordable at the place we crossed in coming. We had to go some miles higher up, and here the swollen rushing waters looked anything but inviting, but after our oratorical friend had made a speech to the river, and rated it for its bad taste in treating visitors, and a white lady too, so badly, we managed to wade across all right.

During our stay at Tabure we made a second visit to the falls when the river was somewhat higher than on the first occasion.

We saw a good deal of the natives; they all look upon us as their friends. They are a good specimen of the average Koiarian. They are somewhat darker in colour and smaller in stature than the coast tribes. They are more hairy too. It is no uncommon thing to see a man with beard and moustache. They are remarkably honest. Mr. Goldie, a botanical and naturalist collector, had his camp for some months in this district, and although there were knives, hatchets, &c., continually lying about, nothing at all was stolen. Like all the other tribes, they are exceedingly superstitious, but their superstition takes a peculiar and most unfortunate form. When a man is ill and dies, he is supposed to be bewitched and not diseased. Almost all the tribes have this belief, but the Koiarians go farther than others. They always know whose spirit has bewitched their friend, and the tribe to whom the spirit belongs has to pay for it. The deceased would not be able to rest until one of that tribe is killed to pay for his death. Whenever a man of the least consequence dies there is always fighting. Tribes that have been on the most friendly terms become enemies on this account alone. We succeeded in preventing fighting during our visit in the case of a tribe who had lost a man through some bad spirit belonging to the Sogere tribe.

Their mode of getting fire is peculiar. They get a dry stick of pithy wood and split it a little way. In the cleft they put a piece of wood or a stone to keep it open, then putting a little rubbish as tinder under the split part of the stick, they stand on the other end and pass a strip of rattan cane or bamboo under the cleft, drawing it rapidly up and down, when it soon begins to smoke, and a spark appears between the fork of the stick, which with a little careful manipulation sets fire to the tinder and a flame is soon obtained. It seems to me easier and quicker than the common way of getting fire with two sticks.

Food is very plentiful in these mountain regions. The gardens, made on the sides of breakneck gullies, are very productive. They grow splendid sugar-cane, a great variety of bananas, and plenty of taro and yams. Breadfruit trees are plentiful, but the fruit is small and full of seeds—very poor after the South Sea Islands breadfruit.

The natives have a great craving for salt; no present is more acceptable than a screw of salt, they prefer it to sugar. They eat it alone, but are especially fond of chewing it with green ginger.

We returned home after spending ten days in the mountains. We had walked about 60 miles and ridden 30.

I am sorry that I could not fix the exact positions of the mountain and falls, but our *time* failed us; the pocket chronometer has stopped, and after I had rated my watch it also stopped. All I could do under the circumstances was to get cross bearings with the prismatic compass. I inclose them and also a tracing showing what we suppose to be about the position of the places we visited.

I am, yours sincerely,

The Secretary R. Geogr. Society.   W. G. LAWES.

PROCEEDINGS OF FOREIGN SOCIETIES

Geographical Society of Paris.—April 20th, 1883, first General Meeting of the year: M. FERDINAND DE LESSEPS in the Chair.—The Meeting was chiefly occupied with the distribution of the prizes awarded by the Society. On the platform, besides the members of the Bureau, were the Mexican Minister at Paris, and a member of the United States Embassy, representing M.'Morton, who was prevented from attending. Delegates were sent also by the Ministers of the Army, Navy, and Public Instruction respectively.—The Chairman opened the meeting with a speech, in which he recalled the fact that it was now fifty-four years since the Society made its first awards. Since that time 153 prizes had been awarded, of which 86 had been made to Frenchmen, and among these M. de Lesseps had the pleasure of being able to reckon himself. On the present occasion three of the awards were conferred upon Frenchmen, and for works having Africa as their object. Speaking of Africa M. de Lesseps stated that he had only just returned from that continent, and that he had visited it in order to consider on the spot the project of an inland sea in the Sahara. He was convinced that the scheme was practicable, as he had stated in the report which he had presented, since his return, to the Academy of Sciences, and that most happy results would follow from the creation of this inland sea.—M. William Hüber, General Secretary of the Commission of Prizes, then read his report, after which the medals were distributed as follows:—one to Commander Gallieni, for his mission to Sego-Sikoro (1880-1); another to Commander Derrien for his topographical mission to Senegal (1880-1); a third to M. Charles Hüber for his journey in Arabia (1879-82); the "Roquette" prize to M. F. Schwatka, the American lieutenant, for his voyage to King William's Land; and the "Erhard" prize to M. A. D. Langlois, for his maps of the department of Oran. Up to the present time it had been the practice of the Society, in making its awards, to recognise a mission in the person of its chief, at the same time giving due praise to his colleagues in the report; hence it has been the commander only who has received and kept the medal. In future the Society will give to each member of the mission a bronze medal, bearing a special inscription, which will be a reproduction of the gold medal awarded to the mission in the person of its commander. Speaking of M. Charnay's recent journey, and of his archæological discoveries in Yucatan, the Secretary stated that the Commission regretted its inability to recognise their value by a medal this year, the results of the journey not being as yet embodied in a printed work (which is a *sine quâ non* condition, according to the Society's rules). M. Charnay's journey had been largely supported by M. Pierre Lorillard (of New York), a descendant of a French family, which took refuge in Holland in consequence of the revocation of the Edict of Nantes, and then emigrated to America. From the report of M. Hüber it appeared that this generous patron of many scientific enterprises and charitable works is now instituting a prize of 1000*l.* (25,000 francs) to the man who will be the first to decipher the inscriptions engraved on the monuments which M. Charnay has brought from Yucatan.—The reports upon the journeys which had merited prizes were then read by the various secretaries, MM. H. Duveyrier, H. de Bizemont (requested by M. Maunoir), Comte de la Turenne, Schrader, and Dunan.—On behalf of the Gallieni mission it was stated that its geographical work may be divided into four sections. (i.) The exploration of the district lying between Bafulabé and Kita. (ii.) The examination of the course of the Baula, from the ford of Tukoto on the Bakhoy to Sambabugu, and also of the country which extends from this latter point to Marena. (iii.) The survey of Birgo and of Manding, together with the exploration of the route from Kita to Niagassola and Nafadia. (iv.) The exploration of the country from Kita by the Bélédugu and Bammaku to Sego. The map prepared by the mission just completes that of Western Soudan, by Mage (1868). The last part of the geographical work of M. Gallieni and his colleagues consisted in preparing accurately a map of the district which lies along the right bank of the Niger, between the ford of Turella and Nango, a region which Mage's account has already made sufficiently well known.—The object of the Derrien mission was to execute a reconnaissance of the Upper Senegal and the Upper Niger, and to find a simple and economical route for a railway between the two rivers. From the observations which the mission has made, it appears that there is no serious obstacle to the execution of this great enterprise. From Kayes to Bafulabé the survey of the land has already been made ; from this latter point to Kita, instead of skirting the Bakhoy, whose banks are very uneven, it is proposed to follow the route traversed by the mission on its return, and along which, for a distance of 135 miles (217 kilometres), only one hill is encountered. Moreover, the ground there is protected from inundations, and the inhabitants are peaceable. Between Kita and Bammaku M. Derrien, in accordance with information obtained from the natives, recommends the route which follows the valley of the Bakhoy, then that of the Kumakhana river, in order to descend to the Niger by the hill of Sanamorila and the valley of the Amarakoba. By this route the railway will command the great market of Keniera, near the gold-mines of Buré; it will pass through the friendly peoples of Manding, and it will follow the caravan route. A map showing the journeys of MM. Derrien and Gallieni in the kingdom of Sego had been passed round at the commencement of the meeting.—Another map, which was also supplied to the audience, showed the travels of M. Charles Hüber in Northern Arabia and in the Syrian desert (1879-82). The route followed by the traveller is not altogether new. M. Wallin (1848), Mr. Palgrave (1862), M. Guarman (1864), M. Doughty (1876-8), M. and Mme. Blunt (1878-9), had already made journeys more or less long in the country, and trodden almost all the ground which M. Hüber must have traversed. But geography occupied but a secondary place in their thoughts, and it would have been useless, says M. Duveyrier, for any one to try and disentangle from their accounts either the great fundamental features of the physical geography of the North of Arabia, or to obtain any data, however scanty, from which to prepare a map of it. M. Hüber's journey just supplies these deficiencies. It throws an altogether new light upon our knowledge of the geography of Northern Arabia, of its past civilisation, and of the present habits of the representatives of the Wahabite power.—After the reading of all the reports and the distribution of the medals, M. Bouquet de la Grye (Hydrographical Engineer and Vice-President of the Central Commission) gave an account of his recent voyage to Mexico, where he went to make observations upon the transit of Venus, a phenomenon which will not be seen again either during this century or the next; four generations will have to pass away before it occurs again. It was at Puebla that the French mission studied the phenomenon. M. B. de la Grye described this town, the installation of the French observations at Fort Loreta, and the astronomical observations made on the 6th of December, 1882, which were a complete success. At other stations the astronomers were not so fortunate.—In conclusion, the results of the ballot for the election of the Bureau of the Society (1883-4) were announced: President, M. de Lesseps, re-elected; Vice-Presidents, M. Maltebrun and M. H. Duveyrier; Secretary, M. D. Charnay. (The scrutineers were M. L. Vignes and M. P. Mirabaud.)

———— May 4th, 1883: M. ANTOINE D'ABBADIE (of the Institute) in the Chair. —M. de Bernardières, naval lieutenant, who has been to Chili on a scientific mission (the observation of the transit of Venus) had written from Buenos Ayres, on his arrival there, to the effect that two of the men who formed part of the Crevaux mission, viz. the boatswain, a Frenchman named Haurat, and an Argentine sailor of the name of Blanco, are still alive and prisoners among the Indians. This news has been forthwith communicated to the French press. M. de Bernardières further states in his letter that he has been commissioned by Dr. Estan. Zeballos, President of the Argentine Geographical Institute, to send to the Society the originals of some astronomical observations taken by Crevaux, particularly affecting the geographical positions of Salta and Jujuy, the capitals of two provinces of the same names in the Argentine Republic. These positions had not previously been scientifically determined. In a letter dated March 21st, Dr. Zeballos states that a fresh expedition of a military character, and organised by the Argentine Government, had just started for the Pilcomayo. It is commanded by Colonel Sola, commander-in-chief on the frontiers of the Grand Chaco, and is composed of 200 men from the regular army. Its object is to surround the Indians in their forest retreats and to obtain the release of Haurat and Blanco. On the way Colonel Sola will endeavour to solve the geographical problem concerning the existence of a new river in the Chaco, the Teyo, a river running parallel with the Pilcomayo. — M. Alph. Milne-Edwards (of the Institute), Professor of the Natural History Museum, who is going to undertake a fresh campaign in the interests of submarine zoology, no longer in the *Travailleur* but in a vessel named *Le Talisman*, announced the 1st of June as the date of his departure. He will sail along the western coast of Africa as far as the Cape Verd Islands, then he will explore the Sargassus Sea, and will finish with a stay at the Azores Islands.—Dr. Colin, naval physician, writes on board *La Gironde* that he has embarked on the mission, with which he is charged, to Buré, to Uassulu and to the other auriferous countries which surround the Upper Niger. He will there collect as much scientific and geographical information as possible. In two months he will be on the Niger, and will take advantage of the rainy season to make excursions into the neighbouring countries. He will return next April twelvemonth.—A letter dated from Uitscha, March 3rd, was received from M. Robert Flegel, the envoy of the German African Society, who for several years has been travelling in the district of the Lower Niger, stating that he had just discovered the sources of the Benué and of the Logona, a tributary of the Shary; he promises to give more complete details later on.—M. Gabriel Marcel, of the Map and Plan Department (National Library), sent a work which he has just published in the 'Scientific Review'; the title of this historico-geographical work is 'Nos droits sur Madagascar.' The book is curious inasmuch as it reproduces a manuscript map which has escaped the notice of M. Grandidier, in spite of the care which the latter has exercised in collecting all the documents relating to this great island. The map shows all that portion of the island subjected to French arms and influence by Flacourt, Mondevergue, &c.— M. P. Schjelderup Nissen, lieutenant of the Norwegian Staff, transmitted a map of Norway in four sheets, scale 1:800,000, prepared by the aid of journeys and information obtained from local authorities, the districts represented not having been as yet the object of topographical surveys. The same correspondent sends also the second edition of a map of South Norway on the same scale in two sheets.—General Mich. Venukoff sent to the Bureau a copy of a work of his on the physico-geographical conditions of the existence and development of the Russian people (published in a Russian review), and at the same time a very interesting account of the Exhibition recently opened at the Winter Palace in St. Petersburg. The Exhibition contains the works in connection with astronomy, geodesy, topography, and geography undertaken and executed in Russia during the year 1882, and not only in Russia but also by Russians in Turkey, Persia, Independent Turkistan, Dzungaria, Mongolia, and Manchuria. M. Venukoff enumerates the documents which appear to him to offer the most interest in this collection. His communication will be inserted *in extenso* in the report of the meetings.—The same will be done in the case of a letter, sent by M. Romanet du Caillaud upon the administrative divisions of Tong-king, and on the difficulty of accurately computing its population. The author has drawn his information especially from ' Le Correo Sino-annamita,' a work compiled with the aid of letters of Spanish Dominican missionaries. Upon this authority the population of Tong-king would be more than 18 millions (Central Tong-king, 4 millions; East Tong-king, 5 millions; West Tong-king, 7,800,000; South Tong-king, 2 millions). The same correspondent sends some information on that part of the West Coast of Africa, against the occupation of which the Portuguese, i. e. the newspapers, have recently protested, viz. Ponta-Negra, of which M. de Brazza and his company are announced as having taken possession. This locality is 68 miles (110 kilometres) distant from Malemba, the extreme point of the " theoretical " possessions of the Portuguese. The writer refers to the map of the coast of Loango and of the Congo, published by Père Duparquet in 1875, in which are indicated with their nationalities the different European factories of the coast. Lastly a third communication from M. Romanet du Caillaud consists of an account of the relations of the Portuguese and the French, which, he says, ought to be more intimate. Indo-China being full of the fame of the glories of Portugal, our correspondent asks the Society to fall in with a wish that he has formed, viz. that France should give the names of Portuguese travellers either to various points of Annam still unnamed, or to the streets of Saigon, or to French concessions at Hanoi, at Haiphong, &c. This desire will be transmitted to the Central Commission.—A note was received from M. Severtsof on the ancient routes across Pamir, together with a manuscript map.*—The French chargé d'affaires at Stockholm and the French Minister at Copenhagen sent some information on the fresh voyage which M. Nordenskiöld is undertaking to Greenland. At the same time a Danish expedition is to visit the eastern coast and prepare a map of it. It will also study the extent and movements of the great masses of ice in these latitudes. This latter expedition will remain several years in the country.—It was announced that a society has been organised for a trip to Norway and Spitzbergen in 1883, the cost of tickets being 100l. sterling. The company transmitted an Anglo-French prospectus announcing that the departure will take place from Havre at the beginning of June. " Proceeding thence direct to Christiania . . . then along the west coast of Norway, stopping especially at Cape North and Hammerfest. From Hammerfest the steamer will proceed as far as Spitzbergen, passing by Bear Island."—The General Secretary then stated that the Royal Geographical Society of London had just awarded the Back Prize for 1883 to M. l'Abbé Petitot, the missionary who has lived for so many years in the midst of the ice of Canada.—M. Letaille, who has returned from Tunis, presented to the Society some photographs, a map, with three itineraries, as well as the inscriptions which he has discovered, and regarding which he will shortly speak before the Society.—M. Emile Guiard, brother of one of the

---

* See the quarterly *Bulletin* of the Society.

victims of the Flatters mission, stated that in his opinion the inauguration of a monument recently erected at Uargla to the memory of the unfortunate travellers was not sufficiently imposing, and he went on to compare to this, an almost private ceremony, the respect paid by the English to the remains of Gill and Palmer, which were interred in Westminster Abbey, their murderers being apprehended scarcely two months after the crime. He demanded the punishment of the murderers of the Flatters mission, who are known at Insalah.—In conclusion, M. Mosenthal, Consul of the Orange River Republic at Paris, read a paper on the Island of Cuba.*

Geographical Society of Stockholm.—February 16th, 1883: the President, Dr. O. MONTELIUS, in the Chair.—The Meeting accepted Baron Nordenskiöld's proposition to confer the *Vega* medal on Mr. Stanley. This distinction, which the Society may confer on men who are distinguished for their geographical researches, and which has been instituted in honour of the *Vega* expedition, has only been twice before awarded, viz. in 1881 to Baron Nordenskiöld, and in 1882 to Captain Palander.—Dr. H. Stolpe read a paper on the ethnography of the Pacific islands. He selected on this occasion Easter Island, referring to its position, discovery, and the former visits of Cook, La Peyrouse, and Kotzebue, and the more recent journeys, in 1868, of Palmer, and in 1877 of Pinart. The most remarkable recent discovery in the island was a number of rough stone figures, representing human heads and busts without arms or legs. Two were found in the bottom of a volcanic crater and some on the coast. Some bore inscriptions, which had, however, not yet been interpreted. The natives referred them to pre-historic inhabitants. Other remains such as sepulture vaults and carved wooden boards, bespoke a high pre-historic culture. The speaker urged a close examination of these relics.—Dr. H. Hjärne next gave an account of the Russians as a colonising people. Having traced the outlines of the Russian conquests in the East, he pointed out the remarkable fact, that the Sclave, when assimilating with the races of Siberia, gradually becomes Siberian both in religion and habits. The most remarkable statement by the speaker was, however, that since the emancipation the Russian peasants have shown a distinct tendency to wander eastwards, which the Government do everything to counteract.

———— March 16th, 1883: the President, Dr. O. MONTELIUS, in the Chair.—The first who addressed the Meeting was Baron v. Düben, who stated that, in consequence of M. Rogozinsky's journey to Africa not having taken place, one of the members of the expedition, the Swedish traveller, Captain T. C. Een, had joined Mr. Stanley on the Congo. He would, whilst in Africa, make collections for the National Museum.—Herr R. Arpi next gave an account of Iceland, chiefly ethnographical, as studied during his journeys there in 1881 and 1882.—Captain A. Fries exhibited and described the utensils used in South and Central America for drinking "maté," while lastly Consul Elfving gave an account of Mr. O'Donovan's journey to Merv.—At this meeting a model of a group of fishing Chukches was exhibited which are intended for the International Fisheries Exhibition in London. It consists of a man and a woman, the former standing, with an ice "bill" in his hand, and the latter sitting, with a rod in her hand. Both dresses and weapons were brought home in the *Vega*, with other articles. The faces of the figures were sculptured by Herr Hyllengren, and painted by Miss Westfelt, and the whole arranged by Miss Pålman from a drawing in Nordenskiöld's ' Voyage of the *Vega*.'

———— April 24th, 1883: the President, Dr. O. MONTELIUS, in the Chair.—King Oscar, the Crown Prince, and the Duke of Vestergötland were present at the

———

* See the quarterly *Bulletin* of the Society.

meeting, which was held on the anniversary of the return of the *Vega*. The meeting opened by the Chairman handing the *Vega* medal, conferred on Mr. Stanley, to the United States Minister in Stockholm, Mr. Stevens, who thanked him for the honour conferred upon his countryman.—Baron Nordenskiöld next gave an account of his intended expedition to Greenland. The speaker said that soon after the return of the *Vega* a rumour went forth, that a new Arctic expedition was about to be equipped, and that the object of the journey was this time the New Siberian Islands. At that time it was really his intention to have visited these islands where so many interesting problems still remain to be solved, taking his expedition by way of the river Lena. In the meantime circumstances, however, caused him to abandon this plan, as several of the explorations he had in view had been effected by the unfortunate *Jeannette* expedition, while, by the search-expeditions despatched to relieve De Long, the delta of the Lena had also been explored in every direction, and eventually it was decided to establish a Russian observatory at the mouth of this river as part of the international programme of observation. It therefore appeared to him that the time for an expedition to the New Siberian Islands was not suitable, and he turned his attention instead to another polar land, where just as important problems remained to be solved, viz. Greenland. Greenland was discovered nine hundred years ago, viz. in 983, by the Norwegian Erik Röde, and its discovery caused at the time great excitement in North Europe. Several colonies were founded there, which flourished so well, that they numbered about 300 farms or "Gaarde," of which 200 were in the so-called "Osterbygd," and 100 in the "Vesterbygd." By degrees the voyages of the Norwegians to Greenland ceased, probably owing to the circumstance that the trade there became a Government monopoly, and to the "black pest," which devastated Norway. At last the colonies were forgotten in the mother-country, and it was only through Columbus' discovery that attention was recalled to them. The attempts which were made to reach Greenland, were, however, long unsuccessful. The south-east coast, where the Osterbygd was believed to have stood, being nearest Iceland, was found to be so closely girt by drift-ice that no vessel could reach it, and this has in fact been the case ever since, although, of course, vessels have reached the coast further to the north. During the attempts which were made in the sixteenth century to find the north-west passage, it was however discovered that the west coast was easily reached ; but colonies were not founded here until the eighteenth century, when the Norwegian, Hans Egede, with the object of finding and converting his old countrymen, settled among the Esquimaux on the west coast. At present there are a number of Danish colonies on this coast from Cape Farewell to Upernivik, lat. 73°. Through the researches of Danish and Swedish *savans* the west coast of Greenland had become one of the best known countries in the Arctic regions. This was, however, far from being the case with the east coast and the whole of the interior. It has been assumed by travellers that the extensive glaciers which are encountered along the coast, and which form an ice plateau 3000 to 6000 feet high, from which ice is precipitated through certain fiords into the sea, cover the entire country. The example of Greenland has been advanced as a proof that a part of the globe was during the last geological age covered with ice. But during his journey along the coast of Siberia, where the climate is far more severe than in Greenland, and also from subsequent researches, he had come to the conclusion that provided there do not exist causes in the interior for the formation of ice, of which we are not aware, it was a physical impossibility that Greenland could be entirely covered with ice. His reasons for this assumption were that all winds which reach Greenland must have passed the sea and thus be moist. Now, when such a wind passes a mountain ridge, it assumes the properties of the Fohn wind, i.e. after having passed the mountains it is dry and

2 B 2

warm.   If the orographical condition of Greenland now was such that the country
rose gradually from the coast on all sides this theory would be untenable, but as it
is improbable that this country is entirely different from all others on the globe, and
that valleys and plains must exist here in the interior, it is evident that all winds
reaching the interior must have the properties of the Fohn wind, i.e. are dry and
somewhat warm.   The conditions for a "permanent" ice formation he believed could
therefore not exist in Greenland, and the interior was most probably free from ice.
The solution of this problem was the chief object of the expedition, while it would
no doubt also be fruitful as regards geography and geology.   More than one chapter
in the chief works on geology would have to be re-written if it should be proved
that his assumption was true.   There were besides many other important scientific
problems to be solved by this expedition.   Of these there was the sea between
Reikiavik and Cape Farewell, which is very little known, as well as the sea west of
Greenland, known less still.   Dredgings and hydrographical soundings of these seas
would therefore, no doubt, give great scientific results.   Another object was the fine
dust which he had on many occasions examined, and which is found in small quantities on the snow and ice in polar regions, a phenomenon of great scientific interest,
as the dust had been found to contain metallic iron, nickel, and cobalt, and was thus
shown to be of cosmic origin.   It was to be hoped that the expedition would, during
its progress along the ice between Reikiavik and Cape Farewell, be in a position to
search for such dust.   The polar countries, whose climate is now so inhospitable,
had, during the geological period nearest to our own, viz. the tertiary, quite different
conditions of temperature.   As an example of this he might mention that of the trees
which form the principal vegetation of Texas, viz. *Taxodium distichum*, fossil remains
were found in large quantities in Spitzbergen.   In Greenland too there were numerous signs of a previous rich vegetation, which had been fully demonstrated by
early investigators, as well as by himself in 1870.   As one of the most celebrated students of fossil palæontology, Dr. A. G. Nathorst, would accompany
him on his expedition, he felt sure that even here important discoveries would be the
result.   In 1870 he had discovered the well-known iron blocks on Disco Island, which
had caused such an active scientific controversy, as to whether they were of terres-
trial or meteoric origin, which latter theory he defended himself.   This discovery
is however, not the only one of its kind in Greenland; Ross and Sabine had found
some similar blocks at Cape York, lat. 76°, where they were used by the Esquimaux
to make their utensils and weapons from.   This subject it was also his intention
to investigate; while he was away on the inland ice, the vessel with the other
members of the expedition would steam to Cape York, and attempt to solve the
problem, and during the journey there would also be a good opportunity of studying
the botanical and palæontological features of these almost unknown parts, and make
collections.   No Scandinavian expedition to Greenland should lose sight of the
problem: Where were the old Norse colonies situated?   This had never been
decided.   From the circumstance that it had never been possible to penetrate the
ice-barrier on the east coast, a Danish savant had come to the conclusion that the
Osterbygd had never been situated here, but had been founded on the south-west
coast where the Vesterbygd lay, a little further north.   Against this assertion he
could advance several objections.   Firstly, he considered it strange, that the old
Norsemen who sailed far and wide, should in Greenland have made such a great
mistake as to the points of the compass, and secondly, he thought that the very
insignificant remains found on the west coast could not be those of the magnificent
buildings to which reference was made in the Sagas, even if the descriptions there
were a little exaggerated.   He considered, therefore, that there was much in favour
of his belief that these colonies had lain on the east coast, and to decide this was also

one of the objects he had in view in the coming expedition. The following was the programme he had drawn up. The vessel would leave Gothenburg on May 20th, while he himself would join her some days later at Thurso, where she would call for coals. From here she would go to Reikiavik, perhaps calling at Rödefjord on the south coast of Iceland to land a Swedish naturalist, and to collect some of the splendid minerals which are to be found here. In Reikiavik, the stay would only be for a few days for coaling. From here she would make for the ice-belt in the west, without, however, attempting to penetrate the same, which all experience had shown to be futile. After having passed Cape Farewell, dredging the sea, the vessel would go to Ivigtuk on the west coast of Greenland, which is a spot of mineralogical interest, as here are found large masses of the rare mineral "kryolit" as well as other kinds. The next place visited would be the Auleitsivik fiord, from which he and Professor S. Berggren had in 1870 made the excursion on the inland ice. He intended to make this spot his starting-point also on this occasion, and his journey would, he estimated, last thirty to forty days, the land party consisting of ten in all. While he was absent, the party on board would make hydrographical researches in Davis Strait, and examine the iron blocks at Cape York already referred to. When the trip to the inland ice was ended, the vessel would steam to Ivigtuk to coal, and the expedition to the east coast be effected. In September he expected to find an ice-free channel along this coast. On his return voyage his course would be outside the ice. The expedition was patronised by the King, and the Government had placed the steamer *Sophia* at its disposal, which vessel on account of her construction, with water-tight compartments, a powerful engine, and being of handy size, would be very suitable, as there was no intention of forcing the ice. The expenses of the expedition would be borne by Dr. Oscar Dickson, and the members of the same would be: Dr. Nathorst, palæontologist; Dr. Berlin, physician; Messrs. Forstrand and Kolthoff, zoologists; and Dr. Hamberg, hydrographer. The vessel would be commanded by Captain Emil Nilsson, who was an experienced Arctic skipper, while a Norwegian hunter, Herr Johannesen, and a Norwegian harpooner would accompany her as ice-masters. The total number of men would be twenty-four. The expedition was intended to return to Sweden in October next, and he, the commander, was certain that the journey was not in the least attended with danger, and that there was no fear of being frozen in, and thus compelled to winter. The number of nautical miles covered by the vessel would be :—Gothenburg to Thurso 500, Thurso to Reikiavik 700, Reikiavik to Ivigtuk 870, Ivigtuk to Auleitsivik fiord 540, Auleitsivik fiord to Omenak 330, Omenak to Cape York 400, viz. a total of 3340 nautical miles.

Société Khédiviale de Géographie, Cairo.—March 23rd : Nahdi Pasha, Governor of the Harrar, gave some particulars of that region from personal knowledge. As he could only address the Meeting in Arabic, his remarks were translated into French, and the following notes placed on the records of the Society :—There are two roads from Zeila to Harrar, the summer one through Tokoscia, Ambos, and Abasuen; the winter one, to the eastward, through Warabat, Mandaa, and Eusa. They unite at a point less than midway, and form but one road through Biakabonba, Kotto, Garasli, and the Gildessa Pass. This information corresponds with that contained in Giulietti's map of 1879, published by Guido Cora in his 'Kosmos,' with the exception that the latter shows "Ellan" in both the winter and summer road, whereas the Pasha's notes, as translated, make it at the point of junction. From Zaila to Gildessa the distance is ten days for camels doing seven hours a day ; and twelve days for those marching six hours. From Zeila to Ellan is ten days; from Gildessa to Harrar, two days. The professional camel-men are "Issas," but at Gildessa, where the territory of the Gallas begins, they leave the traveller, who has to hire horses and camels from the latter people. There are no military stations along the road, those of Ensa, Summedo, and Abasuen having been abolished. But the sheikhs of the several camping-grounds are responsible for the safety of travellers. No mishap ever occurs; merchants and others traverse the country with one or two camels, unattended save by two or three servants, and large sums of money are conveyed from Harrar to Zeila, and *vice versâ*, by simple messengers. It is, of course, to be understood that wages and hire are duly paid for service rendered. There is a road, besides, leading from Harrar tò Berbera. This very difficult and very mountainous track passes through a country inhabited by the Somali Habaroni, who do not bear a good reputation. The journey is of sixteen days, of which four are without water; it is performed on donkeys and mules only. The country between Zeila and Harrar is generally sterile, little frequented, and little known. It is inhabited by nomad tribes. At Harrar itself and in the immediate neighbourhood, it is very fertile, cultivated, and well known. Each tribe of Gallas has its territorial limits clearly defined. The inhabitants are skilful workmen and industrious; they cultivate coffee and other plants, and work tolerably in iron and brass. Nominally Mussulmans, they are not, except in the towns, attentive to their religious duties. As to morals they are rather highway robbers than petty thieves. The priests and sheikhs of Harrar speak Arabic. Commerce is carried on by money payments and exchanges in kind, such as Venetian glass, Paris jewelry, and bits of brass or copper. There are several Europeans in Harrar, some twenty Greek merchants, four French Jesuits, one French and one Italian mercantile house. Nahdi Pasha concluded his remarks by inviting European travellers to Harrar and the country of the Gallas, pointing out that they were preferable to the dangerous and unhealthy regions of the Soudan and Central Africa. Security was to be found there, together with much matter of interesting research. He would be delighted to prove personally useful to new comers as he had been to former visitors and merchants; and he hoped to entertain there, at some time, members of the Khedivial Geographical Society. Two Arabic maps were exhibited and referred to by the speaker who, although he scarcely added any new information to that contained in the intelligent and exhaustive notes of Colonel Muhammad Mukhtar Bey, taken in 1876, deserves credit for so readily supplying the Cairo scientific public with the results of his experience in the Harrar and adjoining tracts.

—— April 20th: Dr. Abbate Pasha in the Chair.—A paper was read by Mr. Whitehouse, giving an account of recent explorations in the Faiyúm, chiefly with a view to determine the true position of the Lake Mœris. His argument against its identification with the " Birkatu-l-Karún " had already been intelligibly put about a year ago, and is to be found in the ' Proceedings of the Society of Biblical Archæology,' dated 6th June, 1882. On the present occasion Mr. Whitehouse went into his subject in considerable detail, and readily answered the interrogatories put to him by one or other of his auditors.

NEW BOOKS.

(By E. C. Rye, *Librarian* R.G.S.)

EUROPE.

Bædeker, Kar —Griechenland. Handbuch für Reisende. Leipzig (Karl Bædeker): 1883, 12mo., pp. cxxii. and 371, maps, plans, panorama of Athens, and other illustrations. (*Dulau*: price 7s. 6d.)

This first issue on Greece by the well-known Leipzig publisher is based on 10 years' actual travel and observation by Dr. Lolling of Athens, with additions on Olympia by Dr. Dörpfeld and Dr. Karl Purgold, and on various archæolological points connected with the museums in Sparta, Piali (Tegea), and Dimit-zana, &c., also by the latter authority. Contributions from other sources are also acknowledged, and Dr. Reinhard Kekulé has given an historical treatise on Greek Art, which with the other ethnological and chronological matter in the voluminous introduction removes the work above the usual guide-book type. The maps are of the whole kingdom (loose in cover), from Kiepert's new Hand-Atlas, scale 1 : 1,000,000, showing steamer lines (also reduced for easy reference on the cover at end); a general sketch of routes in South-eastern Europe, Asia Minor, and North Africa, scale 1 : 6,000,000; Corfu, scale 1 : 300,000; Athens and its vicinity, scale 1 : 150,000; the Piræus, scale 1 : 25,000; Mycenæ, scale 1 : 9400; the plans are of Athens, the Acropolis, and Olympia.

—— West- und Mittel-Russland. Handbuch für Reisende. Leipzig (Karl Bædeker): 1883, 12mo., pp. lii. and 442, maps and plans. (*Dulau*, price 10s.)

Also a new country for the series. In this case, the original groundwork is by Herr Pauli, a captain in the Prussian Artillery, long resident in Russia. A Geographical and Historical section is given in the Introduction, with a short list of books on the country. The maps are of the Warsaw Government, scale 1 : 2,000,000; the vicinity of St. Petersburg, scale 1 : 380,000; the Volga from Nishni-Novgorod to above Samara, scale 1 : 1,000,000; and Central Russia, scale 1 : 8,000,000. The plans are of Warsaw, its inner city and suburbs; Riga; St. Petersburg, inner city and the Eremitage; Helsingfors; Moscow, with the Kremlin; and Nishni-Novgorod.

—— Italy. Handbook for Travellers, by K. Baedeker. Third Part: Southern Italy and Sicily, with Excursions to the Lipari Islands, Malta, Sardinia, Tunis, and Corfu. Eighth revised edition. Leipsic (Karl Baedeker) and London (Dulau): 1883, 12mo., pp. xlviii. and 404, 24 maps, 16 plans. Price 6s.

Revised and augmented, especially as regards Naples, on the climatic and sanitary conditions of which some new and trustworthy notes are given. Some new maps and plans are also given.

Hare, Augustus J. C.—Cities of Southern Italy and Sicily. London (Smith, Elder, & Co.): 1883, post 8vo., pp. viii. and 535, woodcuts. Price 12s.

This very readable volume happens to come fitly next to the Bædeker last above mentioned. With practical information intended for the use of travellers and tourists, it includes much historical, architectural, and artistic detail of the many objects of interest covered by its title, and some few topographical notes.

ASIA.

Gilmour, [Rev.] James.—Among the Mongols. London (The Religious Tract Society): n.d., cr. 8vo., pp. xv. and 382, map and illustrations. Price 6s.

The author narrates his personal experiences among the Mongol tribes who inhabit the eastern portion of the plateau of Central Asia lying between Siberia and China. Starting from Peking, he first saw the great plain in August 1870, and during most of the intervening years has spent the summer months among the tribes to the west, north, and east of Kalgan, having had the opportunity during the winter months in Peking of meeting Mongols coming to that centre on government duty from nearly all the tribes scattered over the vast extent of desert territory which acknowledges Chinese rule. Knowledge of the language, familiarity with the people, and the author's carefulness of observation and caution of statement, warrant the belief that the information in this book is correct.

It is expressly noted that the Buddhism discussed in it is not the ancient theoretic system, but the modern development, for which the better name would be Lamaism. Some of the engravings are from sketches by a Chinese artist of Kalgan.

Murray-Aynsley, [Mrs.] J. C.—Our Tour in Southern India. London (F. V. White & Co.): 1883, 8vo., pp. 358 [no index]. Price 10s. 6d.

Leaving England at the end of October 1879, the authoress visits (besides various well-known localities) the Coorg territory, Cochin, Travancore, &c., and intersperses her narrative with much historical and architectural matter.

Walker, [Lieutenant-General] J. T.—General Report on the Operations of the Survey of India, comprising the Great Trigonometrical, the Topographical, and the Revenue Surveys under the Government of India, during 1881–82. Prepared under the superintendence of Lieutenant-General J. T. Walker, c.b., r.e., f.r s., &c., Surveyor-General of India. Calcutta (Bengal Secretariat Press): 1883, fo., pp. 1–79 and (1)–(120). Maps and frontispiece.

First of the chief operations carried out during the survey year from 1st October, 1881, to 30th September, 1882, recorded in this Report, is the Triangulation,—especially noteworthy from the fact that the chain of principal triangles known as the Eastern Frontier Series, which in previous years had been carried from Assam through Arakan and British Burma into Tenasserim, has now been brought to a close on a base line of verification at Mergui, thus finishing the principal triangulation of all India on the lines originally marked out by Colonel Everest, and sanctioned by the East India Company.

The completion of this great undertaking has necessitated a brief review of the whole operations, from the commencement in 1800 of the so-called "mathematical and geographical survey" in Southern India by Major Lambton on the recommendation of the Duke of Wellington (then Col. Wellesley), clearly illustrated by two charts, one a skeleton of the principal chains as completed to May 1882, with the proposed secondary triangulations in Upper Burma and down the Malayan Peninsula (192 miles to the inch); the other an index chart to the survey (96 miles to the inch), completed to 1st October, 1882, showing Lambton's network in Southern India, the meridional and longitudinal chains of principal triangles, base lines, spirit-levelling lines, astronomical stations, longitudinal arcs, and secondary triangulations for fixing peaks and the positions of Bangkok and Kandahar.

The Topographical operations have been carried on in continuation of those of the former year in Gwalior and Central India, Khandesh and the Bombay Native States, Bhopal and Malwa, Sylhet, and the Khasi and Garo Hills, Rajputana, Mysore, Kohat, Guzerat, Cutch, Meerut, South Deccan, the Hooghly river region, and Beluchistan,—the general out-turn being 6431 square miles surveyed on the ½-inch, 9081 on the 1-inch, 8627 on the 2-inch, 14 on the 6-inch, and 33 on the 16-inch scales, besides the Forest Survey and the survey of 46 square miles of towns, &c, on scales varying from 6 to 80 inches. The survey of the banks of the Hooghly is being carried on simultaneously with a survey of its bed now in progress under the orders of the Port Commissioners, and is of great importance, as the existing maps are out of date and on much too small a scale for practical utility in this densely populated and valuable riverain tract. In connection with this subject, it is pointed out that the old topographical surveys on which the sheets of the atlas of India on the scale of ¼-inch to the mile were founded, were in reality mere geographical reconnaissances, sufficient for their purpose, but now to be superseded by more elaborate survey operations.

The Mouzawar or Village survey of the Dera Ismail Khan district has been completed and extended into the Thal portion of Muzaffagarh, with an area of 1687 square miles; the Riverain surveys on the Jumna and Ganges have yielded 199 square miles; and the Forest surveys in Rawalpindi, Konkan, Tharawaddy (British Burma), and Khandesh cover 1311 square miles; all on the 4-inch scale. Considerable progress is also recorded in the cadastral surveys, areas of 1385 square miles in the North-West Provinces (Ghazipur, Ballia, Mirzapur, and Tarai districts), 3513 in British Burma (Hanthawaddy, Bassein, Tharawaddy, and Rangoon town districts), and 26 in Assam (Sylhet) being surveyed; whilst the geographical surveys and reconnaissances have resulted in the following additions to the country already mapped :—Burma and Manipur boundary, 1600 miles on the ¼-inch, and 1150 on the ⅛-inch; Kohat frontier, 450 on the ½-inch; Beluchistan, 3240 on the ½-inch and 2420 on the ¼-inch; East Sikkim, 180 on the ½-inch; Nepal, 720 on the ⅛-inch; Tibet, 690 on the ¼-inch; Dardistan, 200 on the ¼-inch; and Kishanganga, 600 miles on the ¼-inch.

As frequently the case in these Reports, the chief geographical interest attaches to the Trans-Himalayan explorations by native travellers, the conspicuous value of whose services is attested by the honourable official mention of the late Pundit Nain Singh, c.i.e., who received the Patron's gold medal of this Society in 1877 for his great journeys and surveys in Tibet and along the Upper Brahmaputra, and whose death occurred during the year recorded; and also by the publication of the award of the two medals placed at the disposal of the Surveyor-General by the International Geographical Congress at Venice in 1881. One of these has been presented to M—— S——, and the other is reserved for presentation to A——k, two of the native explorers whose work will be noticed hereunder. Before referring to these, however, it should be remarked that the extracts from the narrative reports of the executive officers in charge of the survey parties and operations given in the Appendix (such as those of Major Rogers, Major Strahan, Major Carter, Colonel Woodthorpe, Mr. McGill, Major Thuillier, Major Holdich, Colonel Haig, Mr. Jarbo, Mr. Badgley, and Mr. Hennessey), contain a very large amount of geographical information and topographical detail, with some points of ethnological and zoological interest. The somewhat lengthy notes of Mr. Jarbo and Major Badgley are especially to be signalised, as descriptive of little known parts of British Burma.

The recorded work of native explorers is as follows :—

(1) Explorations in and around Badakshán by M—— S——, a Pír or holy man, who in 1877 volunteered his services for geographical purposes, being about to make a journey from Kashmir across the Hindu Kush and Oxus to Koláb, to visit ancestral shrines. After being trained at Dehra Dún by the veteran Nain Singh, he arrived at Yasín, north-west of Gilghit, on December 14, 1878, and was detained there for nine months. In September 1879, he proceeded up the Darkoth valley (where Mr. Hayward was murdered), crossed the Shunder Pass into the Mustanj valley, and entered the valley of Wakhán by the Baroghil Pass, striking the Oxus at Sarhad, and thence following the ordinary route to Faizábád.

Towards the end of February 1880, after a diversion to the south to the Daraim valley, he continued his journey, practically following the western and northern route of the Havildar, mentioned in former reports, to Rustak and Koláb, and again crossing the Oxus at Samti. From Koláb he left the Havildar's route, and proceeded up the Doába valley to Rohát, from which point, having found the Kún-i-Gan Pass into Darwáz impracticable, he retraced his steps nearly to Koláb, and crossed into the Dara Imám valley (nearly parallel with the Doába valley), and having followed it to its head, crossed by the Walwalak Pass into the Oxus valley, following the north bank of the river north-eastwards over ground previously unexplored to Kila Khum, where he re-struck the Havildar's route. This he followed south-east to the junction of the Wanj with the Oxus, when he crossed to the south bank, reaching Varv, where (like the Havildar) he was stopped by native hostilities. Retracing his steps as far back as the Imám valley, he then followed the Nayán to its junction with the Oxus, crossing the latter at Kisht, and ascending the table-land of Shiva by a route hitherto wholly unknown, which took him across central Badakshán into the upper basin of the Oxus, which he struck a little above Kilah Bar Panjah. He now proceeded northwards down the river, passing near Kila Wamar, and once more reaching Varv, by a circuitous south-western detour, thus securing an important link hitherto wanting to complete the course of the Oxus. Returning to Kila Wamar, he went north-east up the Bartang or Murghabi valley to Sarez, its highest inhabited point, finding conclusively that the Bartang rises in the Sarez Pamir, and is not a continuation of the Aksú; the latter river was reported to merge in the Sochan, which joins the Shákh Dara at Yamraj, entering the Oxus above Kilah Bar Panjah. After retracing his steps to the latter place, the explorer followed the Shákh Dara valley south-east, but found the southern passes blocked with sand, necessitating a return. His way back to India was down the Oxus, southwards to Ishkásham, which he had touched on the road to Faizábád, and eastward to the Baroghil Pass, where he visited the Gház Kol Lake, determining its position. Independently of the entirely new ground traversed during this long journey the details supplied combine with previous surveys to furnish a nearly complete delineation of the great bend in the Panjah river in its downward course from Wakhán, before it is known as the Oxus.

This important piece of work is clearly illustrated by a special sketch-map (scale 12 miles to the inch) of the whole region, showing the collecting area of the upper Oxus and its chief tributaries, with its circuitous northern loop through Darwáz—a small piece of its course, some 30 miles between Kisht and Samti, alone remaining to be defined.

(2) Explorations on the frontiers of Sikkim by two natives, illustrated on a map (scale 16 miles to the inch). One of them, Babu D. C. S., attached to the Educational Department, and also trained by Nain Singh, started in 1879 from Jongri, in Sikkim. He crossed the Kanchinjinga range to Yamga-tshal in Nepal, on one of the upper affluents of the Tambur, then taking the route which sometimes skirts, sometimes crosses, the western spurs of Kanchinjinga, and visiting the monastery of Taschichoding near Ginmsar (Hooker's Khamba-chen); he then crossed the formidable Chatang Pass, on the Nepal and Tibet borders, to a plateau at the head of the Zemu river, in Sikkim, and also the easier pass of Chorten Nyima Kang into the Tibetan province of Chang, which he traversed by a route to the west of Khamba Jong, eventually reaching Shigatze, south of the Sanpo.

The work of the other native, G. S. S., is less satisfactory; he ascended the Arun valley, in Nepal, to the Popte water-parting which forms the boundary of Nepal and Tibet, and reached the Tibetan village of Karta, where he was stopped. His information, therefore, is chiefly on routes in Nepal.

Captain Harman has made the most of this explorer's few notes, and in the Appendix supplies a memorandum on the data for the map, which includes also the route of G. M. N., another explorer, from Shigatze to Khamba Jong in 1880, as well as those of former explorers, and some of the results of the work of the Darjeeling survey party (especially that of Mr. W. Robert) in 1879–82. Captain Harman adds a memorandum on the longitude of Shigatze, for which he adopts the position of 88° 54' as the most probable value.

(3) A preliminary account of explorations over an extensive area in Great Tibet, to the north and east of the regions reached by Nain Singh, and made by his pupil and former companion A——k, who returned to Calcutta after an absence of four years so recently that there has not been time for the reduction of his observations, the translation of his journals, or the construction of a map. This persevering traveller contrived not only to secrete and preserve his journals, but also his scientific instruments, notwithstanding that on two occasions he was robbed of the greater part of his property. The brief particulars given in the report are practically the same as those already published in our 'Proceedings' for February . last, pp. 99–101. The chief geographical result of his journey is that it sets at rest the frequently-asked question whether the Sanpo flows into the Irawadi or into the Brahmaputra. If the former, the explorer must (as mentioned in the former notice) have crossed it three times, first between Batang and Sama, secondly between Sama and Alanto, and finally at Chetang. He maintains that he only crossed it in the latter place, and that to the west of his route between Sama and Alanto, there is a great range of hills, forming the water-parting between the affluents of the Sanpo and those of the well-known system of parallel Tibetan rivers which he crossed between Batang and Sama. He is stated to know the Sanpo well, to have crossed it frequently and in various places, and to be satisfied that none of these affluents can possibly be identical with it. A full account of his explorations is stated to be intended to be got ready for publication with maps, probably within six months of the issue of the Report.

Accounts of tidal and levelling operations (including some interesting notes on the results of the earthquake of 31st December, 1881, illustrated by a special chart and two diagrams of curves), and of electro-telegraphic longitude operations are also given; and the account of the business of the several Headquarters includes some valuable technical remarks by Major J. Waterhouse on the work done in the Photographic Branch. The success of this indefatigable officer's scientific labours is well shown by the frontispiece of the Report, which is a view of Kanchinjinga reproduced by his process of heliogravure.

In addition to the maps, &c., above noticed, the Report contains a general map of India, showing the progress of the Imperial Surveys to 1st October, 1882; a map of the Eastern frontier series of triangles from Mergui to Lower Siam (scale 30 miles to an inch); and twenty-one maps illustrating the topographical and other surveys noticed in the text.

AFRICA.

Crozals, J. de.—Les Peulhs. Étude d'Ethnologie Africaine. Paris (Maisonneuve): 1883, 8vo., pp. 271 [no index]. (*Dulau*: price 5s.)

After a general review of the geographical distribution and affinities of the African races, entirely derived from German authorities, the author analyses and discusses in detail all former notices of the Fulahs (known also as Fullos, Foulis, Pholeys, Foulahs, Foulanics, Fellans, Fellatahs, with various other modifications), for the Senegambian representatives of which race he adopts the form 'Peulhs' employed by Hecquard, based on the root of the 'Pullo' of Barth (plural 'Fulbe'). It is considered by Dr. Crozals that such a work as this is practically needed, in the face of the preponderance evidently destined for France in the basin of the Niger and its affluents.

AUSTRALASIA.

Geiseler, —.—Die Oster-Insel. Eine Stätte prähistorischer Kultur in der Südsee. Bericht des Kommandanten S. M. Kbt. *Hyäne*, Kapitänlieutenant Geiseler, über die ethnologische Untersuchung der Oster-Insel (Rapanui) an den Chef der Kaiserlichen Admiralität. Berlin (Mittler & Sohn): 1883, 8vo., pp. 54, map and 21 plates. (*Dulau*: price 3s.)

This report of Commander Geiseler, who in the Prussian gunboat *Hyæna* visited Easter Island on 20–25 September last, is an extract from No. 44 of the Supplementary Papers to the German Marine official publication, and, though naturally of most interest to ethnologists, may be taken as itself supplementing the paper by Mr. J. Linton Palmer in our 'Journal,' vol. xl. p. 167, and the illustrated account by M. Alphonse Pinart in the 'Tour du Monde,' vol. xxxvi. p. 225. The visits of the *Topaz* and *Steignelay* in 1868 and 1877, which afforded opportunities for these two writers, are recorded with others in an introductory note to the report, though the accounts themselves would seem to be unknown to its author.

Commander Geiseler, after giving brief details of daily work during his visit (including the positions of some of the prominent points), discusses more elaborately:—1, the hydrographic and generally interesting features; 2, the prehistoric aspects; and 3, the ethnographical, subdivided under Population (now only 150 souls, of whom 67 are males, 39 females, and 44 children, two-thirds of the whole living at Matavéri, where Mr. Salmon, the representative of the Tahitian firm of Brander & Co., lives), Races and types, Language, Numeral system, and Habits and customs. The latter subdivision is copiously treated under various headings, and with the short vocabulary and anthological fragments and 87 ethnographical objects enumerated and briefly described in the Appendix, will doubtless prove of special value to Prof. Bastian, of the Berlin Museum, at whose desire Commander Geiseler appears to have been detached for this service.

The map laid down by the officers of the Chilian corvette *O'Higgins*, and from which our Admiralty chart is taken, is reproduced here, and stated to be in general points correct. Some few corrections are made in the text (p. 5), and our Admiralty chart is stated to give the soundings for the most part as somewhat less deep than in the original. Two original profiles are also given, with original representations of the curious prehistoric and other objects for which the island is famed, including a sketch of the positions of the ancient stone-houses on the south-west slope of the crater of Rana Káo (or Terano-Kau).

GENERAL.

Nordenskiöld, A. E.—Om Bröderna Zenos Resor, och de äldsta Kartor öfver Norden. Stockholm (Central-Tryckeriet) : 1883, 8vo, pp. 60, maps and facsimile.

This elaborately worked out and admirably executed dissertation was read before the Swedish Academy of Science on 12th April last, and is a part of the distinguished traveller's ' Studier och Forskningar föranledda af mina Resor i Höga Norden,' a popular scientific supplement to the account of the voyage of the *Vega* now in course of publication.

It consists of a Swedish translation of the often discussed account published by Marcolini in 1558 of the travels of the brothers Zeni, chiefly familiar to English readers from the masterly analysis by our late Hon. Secretary, Mr. R. H. Major, in the publications of the Hakluyt Society. The original map of the Zeni is reproduced, with the 1561 version of it by Ruscelli in his edition of Ptolemy, a part of Northern Europe from the Cosmographia, the 1483 world-map of Petrus de Alyaco (Pierre d'Ailly), Northern Europe from Donis's edition of the Cosmographia, Bordone's 1547 Scandinavia, the world-map in the British Museum by Martellus Germanus of (*circa*) 1489, Scandinavia and the world-map from Pedrezano's 1548 edition of Ptolemy, Northern Europe from Olaus Magnus, 1567, Andrea Bianco's 1436 MS. map of the North, the 1532 Bâle ' Typus cosmographicus,' the north-west part of Frisius's 1522 map, and a facsimile in colour of the oldest known map of the North, by Claudius Clavus, with its accompanying descriptive text. This, the first to contain a representation of Greenland, bears the date of 1427, and was discovered by Baron Nordenskiöld himself in a MS. copy of Ptolemy's Cosmographia, preserved in the Municipal Library at Nancy. The author, also referred to as Claudius Cimbricus, appears to have compiled this pre-Columbian chart at the instigation of Cardinal Gulielmus Filiastrus. It includes the north of England, Scotland, Ireland, the Orkneys, Iceland, the Danish and Scandinavian peninsulas (including the Baltic apparently to its head, near which are depicted Stockholm and Gothland, and with its eastern shore), and on the extreme west a part of eastern Greenland (with the sole legend "Gronlandia Provincia"), connected with the extreme north of the Scandinavian peninsula by a mythical shore-line north of the Arctic ocean. In the extreme north of Norway as drawn, but considerably lower down on its western face when the peninsula is turned into its proper position, appears also " Engromelandi," which represents the " Engronelant " of Donis.

A careful analysis of all this material, which represents the existing knowledge at the time of Marcolini's publication of the Zeni narrative, has resulted in the following deductions by Baron Nordenskiöld :—

1. That the map of the Zeni must be based on an old sea-chart of the north, constructed before 1482, and probably brought home from Frisland by Antonio Zeno.

2. That we do not know of any exact copy of the original itself, though we do know of two that are more or less altered, namely the chart of Zeno the younger, printed in 1558 and 1561, and Donis's, printed in 1482. On the first, the old distribution of land and sea has been almost exactly adhered to, but on the other hand it has been adapted to the narrative by the addition of various names which appear in the text, such as the islands of Icaria, Bres, Brons, Trans, Iscant, &c., by making the Ferö and Shetland Islands disproportionately larger, and lastly, by adding longitudes and latitudes, the latter being generally too far north. All these alterations are less decided in the first edition of Donis's chart. Here, however, we find the well-conceived alteration that Greenland has been moved further north, to give it a position more in accordance with later determinations by compass observations, and with the geographical ideas of the time.

3. That if both these charts are not independent compilations from the

original one, the richer and more correct chart of the Zeni, both as to names and details, must be the elder.

4. That the chart of the North which Zeno brought home must be regarded, from a cartographical point of view, as extraordinarily good for the time, almost, indeed, on a par with Andrea Bianco's chart of the Mediterranean.

5. That the chart of the Zeni must give the result of experience gained during repeated voyages in these regions by intelligent seamen, probably before the introduction of the compass in the north.

6. That we must conclude from this, that towards the end of the fourteenth, possibly in the fifteenth century, voyages to the north-western [sic] part of America were much more frequent than is generally supposed.

7. That the old sea-chart which Admiral Zahrtmann saw in the Copenhagen Library, and which could not afterwards be found, was Nicolai Donis's chart, which was printed for the first time in 1482.

8. That the east coast of Greenland at that time was less encumbered with ice than at present, because that now inaccessible coast could then be properly charted.

9. That the younger Zeno has left in the book published by Marcolini a generally truthful sketch of the sojourn of two Venetians with a northern rover, who established himself on one of the Færö Islands, and from thence plundered the neighbouring countries, visiting amongst other places a remarkable monastery, probably situated on the east coast of Greenland, and a harbour situated somewhere on the south coast.

10. That fishermen from the rover's head-quarters were driven by a storm to the mainland of America, and there, in Newfoundland and Canada, saw the remains of small communities originally founded by Europeans ; also that these fishermen were compelled by circumstances to make extensive journeys in the interior of the American Continent, of the social conditions of which they have left some graphic pictures.

Ullrich, Valentin.—Die horizontale Gestalt und Beschaffenheit Europa's und Nordamerika's. Ein Beitrag zur Morphologie beider Erdenräume. Leipzig (Duncker & Humblot): 1883, 8vo., pp. 182. (*Williams & Norgate*: price 4s.)

This treatise on the horizontal configuration and composition of Europe and North America originally appeared in 1882 as an academic lecture before the Bavarian State School. Europe and North America are associated as being geographically two highly organised individuals of the same species, as it were, the latter being practically as much a separate continent as the former.

NEW MAPS.

(By J. Coles, *Map Curator* R.G.S.)

WORLD.

Telegraph Map of the World.—Map of the World showing the Submarine Telegraph Cables manufactured and laid by the Telegraph Construction and Maintenance Company, Limited, together with other Telegraph Lines. Mercator's Projection, Equatorial Scale 16¼° to an inch. F. Le-B. Bedwell, R.N., del. Telegraph Construction and Maintenance Company, Limited, London, 1883.

EUROPE.

ORDNANCE SURVEY MAPS.

Publications issued from 1st to 31st January, 1883.

25-inch—Parish Maps :—

ENGLAND: **Bedford:** Arlesey 9 sheets ; Barton in the Clay 11, and Area Book ; Eversholt 8, and Ar. Bk. ; Harlington 8, and Ar. Bk. ; Higham Gobion 8, and Ar. Bk. ; Milton Bryant 6, and Ar. Bk. ; Potsgrove 6, and Ar.

Bk.; Pulloxhill, Ar. Bk.; Shitlington and Do. (Det., Nos. 7 and 8) 16, and
Ar. Bk.; Streatley 8, and Ar. Bk.; Tingrith 6, and Ar. Bk.; Toddington 16,
and Ar. Bk.; Stotfold 8; Upper Stondon 3, and Ar. Bk.; Westoning 9, and
Ar. Bk.; Woburn 11, and Ar. Bk. **Cornwall**: Quethiock 13; St. Pinnock,
Ar. Bk. **Derby**: Allestree, Ar. Bk.; Quarndon, Ar. Bk. **Gloucester**:
Alderley 7; Beverstone 6, and Ar. Bk.; Hawkesbury 25; Tetbury 15;
Wotton-under-Edge 15; Weston Birt with Lasborough, Ar. Bk. **Mon-
mouth**: Caerwent, Ar. Bk.; Caldicot, Ar. Bk.; Llangattock-Vibon-Avel 11;
Llanvihangel-Ystern-Llewern 8, and Ar. Bk.; Llautrissent, Ar. Bk.; Llan-
frechfa, Ar. Bk.; Llandegveth, Ar. Bk.; Llanvair Discoed, Ar. Bk.; Llan-
dewi-fach, Ar. Bk.; Llanvaches, Ar. Bk.; Parc Grace Dieu, Ar. Bk.; Penhow,
Ar. Bk.; Shire Newton, Ar. Bk.; St. Bride's Netherwent, Ar. Bk.; St.
Maughans, 5; Usk, Ar. Bk. **Norfolk**: Attlebridge 5; Crostwick, Ar. Bk.;
Felthorpe 7; Newton Flotman, Ar. Bk.; Stoke Holy Cross, Ar. Bk. **Shrop-
shire**: Acton Burnell 7; Atcham 14, and Ar. Bk.; Beckbury 8, and Ar.
Bk.; Berrington 11, and Ar. Bk.; Boningale, Ar. Bk.; Cardeston, Ar. Bk.;
Ryton, Ar. Bk.; St. Julien, Ar. Bk.; Wroxeter, Ar. Bk.; Condover, 17;
Cressage 6, and Ar. Bk.; Eaton Constantine 5, and Ar. Bk.; Great Hanwood
4, and Ar. Bk.; Leighton and Do. (Det.) 8; Pontesbury and Ford (Det) 23,
and Ar. Bk. **Suffolk**: Aldeburgh 7; Aldringham with Thorpe 5; Boulge
3, and Ar. Bk.; Brandon (Part of) 10, and Ar. Bk.; Brantham 8; Culpho 4,
and Ar. Bk.; Elveden 13; Eriswell 16; Hazlewood 7; Iken 8; Mildenhall
28; Santon Downham 6, and Ar. Bk.; Sproughton, Ar. Bk.; Stutton 10,
and Ar. Bk; Sudbourne 15.

Index Map:—

Index to the Ordnance Survey of Sussex. (Scale 3 miles to 1 inch.)

Publications issued from 1st to 28th February, 1883.

1-inch—General Maps:—

ENGLAND AND WALES: Sheet 257 (in Outline).

IRELAND: Sheet 163 (Hill-shaded).

6-inch—County Maps:—

ENGLAND: Derby Quarter Sheets 9 S.W.; 10 N.W.; 10 N.E.; 11 S.W.; 12
S.W.; 16 S.W.; 16 S.E.; 17 N.W.; 18 S.E.; 19 N.E. (21 N.E. with
Stafford 1 N.E.); (21 S.E. with Stafford 1 S.E.).

IRELAND: Cavan (revised). sheet 39. Longford (revised), sheets 6, 9, 11, 12,
16, 20, 21, 25.

25-inch—Parish Maps:—

ENGLAND: **Bedford**: Astwick 4 sheets; Campton 4; Edworth 6; Langford
6. **Cornwall**: Cardinham 20; St. Martin 9, and Ar. Bk.; St. Neot 27;
Temple 3. **Derby**: Aston upon Trent 8, and Ar. Bk.; Calke 5; Chellas-
ton 4; Derby Hills Township 4; Doveridge and Do. (Det., No. 1) 9, and Ar.
Bk.; Foremark 7; Marston on Dove, and Rolleston (Det., No. 1) 11, and
Ar. Bk.; Melbourne 9; Repton 12; Scropton 10, and Ar. Bk.; Stanton by
Bridge 7; Swarkeston 5, and Ar. Bk.; Ticknall 10; Weston upon Trent 6,
and Ar. Bk. **Gloucester**: Boxwell with Leighterton 7, and Ar. Bk.;
Broughton Poggs (Det.) 3, and Ar. Bk.; Ozleworth 7; Shipton Moyne 6;
Norfolk: Blofield 7; Colton 4; Easton 6; Great Melton 10; Hainford 7
and Ar. Bk.; Hethersett 8, and Ar. Bk.; Honingham 10; Horstead with
Staininghall 10, and Ar. Bk.; Marlingford 5; Postwick 6; Ringland 7.
Shropshire: Habberley 5; Kemberton 6, and Ar. Bk.; Kenley 5;
Minsterley 8; Pitchford 7, and Ar. Bk.; Posenhall 4; Sheinton 5, and Ar.
Bk.; Stapleton 8, and Ar. Bk.; Uppington 5, and Ar. Bk.; Westbury 22;
Wollaston 12; Wombridge 6, and Ar. Bk.; Wrockwardine and Do. (Det.
Nos. 1 and 2) 19, and Ar. Bk. **Suffolk**: Burgh 6; Grundisburgh 7.

Publications issued from 1st to 31st March, 1883.

1-inch—General Map :—IRELAND : Sheet 113 (Hill-shaded).

6-inch—County Maps :—

ENGLAND : Berks, sheet 41 with Wilts sheet 37 and Hants sheet 1. Hertford, sheet 35. Hertford, sheet 5 with Essex sheets 1, 2, 7, 8. Wilts, sheet 55 with Hants sheet 22. Wilts, sheet 61 with Hants sheet 30.

25-inch—Parish Maps :—

ENGLAND : **Bedford**: Arlesey, Ar. Bk. ; Astwick, Ar. Bk.; Campton, Ar. Bk ; Chicksands Priory, 5 sheets, and Ar. Bk.; Clifton 6, and Ar. Bk.; Clophill 6; Edworth, Ar. Bk.; Henlow 8; Langford, Ar. Bk.; Lower Gravenhurst 4, and Ar. Bk.; Meppershall 6, and Ar. Bk. ; Shefford 2, and Ar. Bk.; Shefford Hardwick 4, and Ar. Bk. ; Silsoe 8 ; Stotfold, Ar. Bk. ; Upper Gravenhurst 7, and Ar. Bk. **Cornwall**: Blisland 16 ; Braddock, Ar. Bk. ; Duloe, Ar. Bk.; Landulph 7; Liskeard, Ar. Bk.; Menheniot, 16; Pelynt, Ar. Bk.; Quethiock, Ar. Bk.; Temple, Ar. Bk. **Derby**: Area Books of the following Parishes :—Calke ; Derby Hills Township; Foremark ; Melbourne; Stanton by Bridge; Ticknall. **Gloucester**: Area Books of the following Parishes :—Alderley ; Hawkesbury ; Ozleworth; Tetbury; Wotton-under-Edge. **Monmouth** : Cwmcarvan, Ar. Bk. ; Gwernesney, Ar. Bk.; Henllys 11, and Ar. Bk. ; Kemeys-Inferior 8; Llanbadock, Ar. Bk.; Llangattock juxta Caerleon 11 ; Llangattock-Vibon-Avel, Ar. Bk.; Llangibby, Ar. Bk.; Llanmartin 5; Llanvihangel Pontymoil, Ar. Bk. ; Malpas 4 ; Newchurch, Ar. Bk.; Penrhôs, Ar. Bk. ; Pen-y-Clawdd, Ar. Bk.; Rockfield 9; St. Maughans, Ar. Bk.; Tredunnock, Ar. Bk. **Norfolk**. Area Books of the following Parishes :—Attlebridge; Barford; Blofield; Bracon Ash ; Carleton Forehoe ; Colton ; Crownthorpe ; Dunston ; East Carleton; Easton ; Felthorpe; Flordon; Great Melton; Hethel ; Honingham; Ketteringham ; Marlingford ; Morton on the Hill; Postwick; Ringland ; Weston Longville ; Wramplingham; Wreningham. **Shropshire** : Area Books of the following Parishes :—Acton Burnell; Condover ; Cound; Habberley ; Leighton and Do. (Det.); Minsterley; Posenhall; Westbury ; Wollaston. **Stafford**: Enville 12, and Ar. Bk.; Himley 7, and Ar. Bk. **Suffolk**: Aldeburgh, Ar. Bk.; Barton Mills 5; Brantham, Ar. Bk.; Burgh, Ar. Bk ; Elveden, Ar. Bk.; Eriswell, Ar. Bk ; Grundisburgh, Ar. Bk. ; Hazlewood, Ar. Bk.; Iken, Ar. Bk.; Mildenhall, Ar. Bk.; Snape 7 ; Sudbourne, Ar. Bk.; Tuddenham 9; Wantisden 6.

Town Plan—scale 1 : 500 :—

ENGLAND : Banbury, 23 sheets.

Index Map—SCOTLAND : Index to the Counties of Perth and Clackmannan. Scale 3 miles to 1 inch.

Schweiz, Kleine officielle Eisenbahnkarte der——. Herausgegeben vom Schweizer. Post- und Eisenbahn-Department. Scale 1 : 500,000 or 6·8 geographical miles to an inch. Lausanne. Price 1s. 6d. (*Dulau.*)

Spain.—Mapa Topográfico de España en escala de 1 : 50,000 or 1·4 inches to a geographical mile. Comienza su publicacion el Instituto Geográfico y Estadistico bajo la direccion del Excmo. Señor Don Cárlos Ibañez é Ibañez de Ibero, Director General. Madrid. Sheets :—No. 604. Villaluenga, No. 606. Chinchon, and No. 629, Toledo.

ASIA.

Bock, Carl.—Originalskizze einer Reiseroute von Bangkok zum Mekóng, aufgenommen und gezeichnet von Carl Bock, 1882. Scale 1 : 4,000,000 or 55·5 geographical miles to an inch. Petermann's ' Geographische Mittheilungen,' Jahrgang 1883, Seite 162. (*Dulau.*)

Cochinchine Française, Carte de la——, réduction de la grande carte de M. Bigrel. Price 2s. 6d. (*Dulau.*)

AFRICA.

West Equatorial Africa.—Uebersichtskarte der neuesten Forschungsreisen im äquatorialen Westafrika. Entworfen und gezeichnet von B. Hassenstein. Scale 1 : 5,000,000 or 66·6 geographical miles to an inch. Petermann's 'Geographische Mittheilungen,' Jahrgang 1883, Taf. 6. Justus Perthes, Gotha. (*Dulau*.)

CHARTS.

Admiralty.—Charts published by the Hydrographic Department, Admiralty, in March and April 1883.

No.		Inches.	
359	m	= 0·32	Japan :—Nagasaki to Karatsu, with the Goto islands. (Plans, Tama no Ura. Hardy harbour. Okushi harbour. Nama Ura.) Price 2s. 6d.
287	m	= 0·24	Borneo, northern part:—From Gaya bay on the west, to Sandakan harbour on the east, including South Banguey channel, and the south-western part of Cagayau Sulu. Price 2s. 6d.
491	m	= various.	West Indies :—Anchorages in Guadeloupe and the adjacent islands—St. Anne anchorage. Port du Moule. St. François anchorage. Port Louis. Basse-Terre. Galet anchorage. Saintes anchorage. Grand-Bourg. Price 1s. 6d.
2864	m	= 1·75	North America, east coast:—Beaufort harbour. Price 1s.
2622	m	= 3·0	Shetland isles:—Fair isle. Price 1s.
844	m	= 3·0	Sea of Marmara:—Erekli bay. Palatia and Mermerjik bays. Rodosto roads. Karabuga bay. Gemlik bay. Mudania roads. Panderma bay. Kalolimno island. Price 1s. 6d.
430	m	= various.	Central America, west coast :—Ports and anchorages—Istapa or Isla Grande bay. Sihuatanejo. Petatlan. Tequepa or Papanoa. Guatulco, Santa Cruz, and Tangola Tangola. Maldonado. Angeles. Sacrificios. Price 1s. 6d.
1048	m	= 0·1	Australia, west coast :—Buccaneer archipelago to Bedout island. (Plan, Beagle bay.) Price 2s. 6d.
613	m	= 0·13	Australia, north coast:—Melville island with Dundas and Clarence straits. (Plan, Vernon islands.) Price 1s. 6d.
1754	m	= 0·24	China:—Ragged point to Wên-chau bay. Price 2s.
1759	m	= 0·24	China :—Wên-chau bay to Kweshan islands. Price 2s.
159	m	= 6·0	South America, west coast :—Puerto del Morro. Cockle cove and approaches. Price 1s. 6d.
548	m	= 3·0	South America, east coast:—Maldonado bay. Price 1s. 6d.
2880	m	= 1·78	North America, east coast :—New Bedford harbour. Price 1s.
438	m	= 4·9	France, north coast :—Boulogne. Price 1s.
2094	m	= 0·8	England, west coast :—Isle of Man. (Plans, Ramsey bay. Douglas harbour. Castletown bay. Port St. Mary. Calf sound. Port Erin. Peel.) Price 4s.

451 Plan added, Ocho Rios bay.
2723 Plan added, Pulo Dama.
2369 Plan added, Pillau harbour.

(*J. D. Potter, agent.*)